A Perfect Gentle Knight

Also by Kit Pearson

The Daring Game

A Handful of Time

The Sky Is Falling

Looking at the Moon

The Lights Go On Again

Awake and Dreaming

This Land: An Anthology of Canadian Stories
for Young Readers (as editor)

Whispers of War: The War of 1812 Diary
of Susanna Merritt

A Perfect Gentle Knight

KIT PEARSON

PUFFIN
CANADA

PUFFIN CANADA

Published by the Penguin Group

Penguin Group (Canada), 90 Eglinton Avenue East, Suite 700, Toronto, Ontario, Canada M4P 2Y3 (a division of Pearson Canada Inc.)

Penguin Group (USA) Inc., 375 Hudson Street, New York, New York 10014, U.S.A.
Penguin Books Ltd, 80 Strand, London WC2R 0RL, England
Penguin Ireland, 25 St Stephen's Green, Dublin 2, Ireland (a division of Penguin Books Ltd)
Penguin Group (Australia), 250 Camberwell Road, Camberwell, Victoria 3124, Australia
(a division of Pearson Australia Group Pty Ltd)
Penguin Books India Pvt Ltd, 11 Community Centre, Panchsheel Park, New Delhi - 110 017, India
Penguin Group (NZ), 67 Apollo Drive, Rosedale, North Shore 0632, Auckland, New Zealand
(a division of Pearson New Zealand Ltd)
Penguin Books (South Africa) (Pty) Ltd, 24 Sturdee Avenue, Rosebank, Johannesburg 2196, South Africa

Penguin Books Ltd, Registered Offices: 80 Strand, London WC2R 0RL, England

First published 2007

1 2 3 4 5 6 7 8 9 10 (RRD)

LIBRARY AND ARCHIVES CANADA CATALOGUING IN PUBLICATION

Pearson, Kit, 1947–
A perfect gentle knight / Kit Pearson.

ISBN 978-0-670-06682-7

I. Title.

PS8581.E386P47   2007   jC813'.54   C2007-902649-4

ISBN-13: 978-0-670-06682-7
ISBN-10: 0-670-06682-6

Visit the Penguin Group (Canada) website at **www.penguin.ca**

Special and corporate bulk purchase rates available; please see
www.penguin.ca/corporatesales or call 1-800-810-3104, ext. 477 or 474

For Lizzie and Gretchen, once my fellow knights,
and for
Joe Mitchell

A Knight there was, and that a worthy man,
That from the moment that he first began
To go on journeys had loved chivalry,
Goodness and honour, freedom and courtesy …
And though he was of high rank, he was wise,
And in his manner meek as is a maid.
He never had to any person said
A word that was not tender, kind and right.
He was a truly perfect gentle knight.

GEOFFREY CHAUCER, *THE CANTERBURY TALES*
(MODERN ENGLISH VERSION BY KIT PEARSON)

A Perfect Gentle Knight

1

Meredith

"Corrie, *please* may I play at your house after school today?"

The bell rang, and Corrie had no time to answer before she and Meredith had to line up silently at the girls' entrance. All afternoon Corrie worried about Meredith's question.

Meredith was a new girl. Most of 6A had been together since grade one. The five girls who had always set the rules in the class—Darlene, Gail, Donna, Sharon, and Marilyn—had already decided that Meredith was to be ignored.

Ever since school had started two weeks ago, Corrie had watched Meredith's eager advances being coolly deflected by the rest of the class. It didn't help that Meredith was plump and wore babyish clothes, that she talked too much and wanted so desperately to be liked.

Meredith had turned to Corrie from the start. She stood by Corrie at recess and chattered at her nervously until the bell rang. Now she acted as if she and Corrie were friends. She walked part of the way home with Corrie, and one day the week before she had even invited Corrie over to her house after school.

Corrie's curiosity had made her accept, even though she didn't need friends. Why couldn't Meredith realize that? The other girls had always respected the barrier Corrie had put up and left her alone. Meredith didn't seem to see that barrier.

The trouble was, Corrie liked Meredith. She liked how she spoke in italics, how her dark eyes shone with enthusiasm, how passionate she was about animals. The Five had come back to school talking about rock and roll, and movie stars. Meredith, like Corrie, wasn't interested in those boring topics.

Most of all, Corrie liked Meredith's tidy, clean house, her room full of books, and her friendly parents. Meredith's mother had offered them milk and chocolate chip cookies, and her father had tenderly bandaged Meredith's scraped knee. They were like parents in a TV show.

Corrie dipped her pen into her inkwell, trying to concentrate on copying the spelling words on the board. This was the third time Meredith had asked to come over. If Corrie kept saying no, Meredith would probably never ask Corrie back to her cozy home.

When the bell rang Meredith caught up with her at the door. "So, can I *come*?"

Corrie shrugged. "I guess so. Is it okay with your mum?"

"Yup! I told her at lunch I was going to your house."

So it was all set. Corrie couldn't help smiling. "Come on," she said. "Let's go and get the twins."

"AND COULD YOU PLEASE ensure that they wash their hands before coming into the classroom?" asked a frazzled-looking Miss Tuck, the twins' grade one teacher. Corrie nodded, trying to get away. Every day Miss Tuck had another complaint about Juliet and Orly. They lost their notices. They wouldn't sit still. Orly galloped around the classroom with a ruler for a sword, and Juliet growled whenever she was asked a question.

Corrie grasped two grimy hands and dragged the twins into the rain, despite their protests that they wanted to play with the class hamster.

"I'm fattening him up," boasted Orly. "I sneaked pieces of my sandwich into his cage. He's going to grow as big as a rat!"

"You're not supposed to feed him—only Miss Tuck does that. He'll get sick if you do. I've told you that, Orly. Why can't you remember? Wait, let me do up your jacket."

But Orly had dashed ahead with Juliet. Both unzipped jackets were half off as the twins jumped into puddles and skimmed their hands along wet hedges.

"They're so *wild*," said Meredith. "Like two little savages!"

"They *are* savages," said Corrie grimly. "They don't listen to any of us except Sebastian. Yesterday afternoon Juliet climbed onto the roof and almost fell off. Sebastian was out. The only way we could get Juliet down was to bribe her with marshmallows. She ate so many she threw up all over the kitchen table."

"Sebastian is the oldest, right?" said Meredith. She was always trying to find out more about Corrie's family.

"Yes, Seb's fourteen and Roz is thirteen."

Meredith's mother had asked Corrie about the rest of the family. So Meredith already knew that Corrie's mother had died three years ago, that her father taught Shakespearean literature at the university, and that a series of daily housekeepers had looked after them.

"What school do Sebastian and Roz go to?"

"Laburnum."

"What's *that*?"

Corrie kept forgetting that Meredith was new to Vancouver. "It's the junior high school. I'll be going there next year—so will you!"

"Junior high, *yuck*! Let's not even *think* about it until we have to!"

Corrie grinned at her. Juliet and Orly raced back with a dead robin. "We can have a funeral!" said Juliet gleefully. Corrie stroked the soft, limp body. Its feathers were already faded. She helped Juliet wrap it in leaves.

"Who takes *care* of the twins?" Meredith asked. "Your dad? Your older sister? The housekeeper? Who washes and dresses them?"

Corrie laughed. "Not my father! He never notices what any of us look like! Roz tries to, but they don't stand still long enough to be washed or have their hair combed. They would for Sebastian, but he forgets. And the housekeeper only looks after the house."

Meredith looked longingly at the twins' tangled hair and torn clothes. "They're almost identical—like Freddie and Flossie in the Bobbsey Twins! They'd look *so* cute in matching outfits. And their hair is so blond, it must be nice when it's washed. Why don't *you* try to clean them up?"

"They aren't dolls!" snapped Corrie. "They're fine the way they are."

Uh-oh. Now maybe Meredith wouldn't like her. Corrie shivered under her sopping jacket. Her feet were soaked as well. There were no boots in the family that fit her, and she kept forgetting to ask Roz to buy her some. She glanced enviously at Meredith's yellow rain slicker and matching yellow boots.

"Sorry, Corrie," said Meredith. "I've *always* wanted a little sister or brother. I was just imagining what I'd do if they were mine. You're so *lucky*!"

"It's okay," muttered Corrie. "I guess they *are* pretty grubby. And sometimes I do try to wash them. But Juliet bites!"

Orly, who'd rushed ahead again, ran back and pinched Meredith. "Monkey tree, no pinchies back!" he shouted.

"Ouch!" Meredith rubbed her arm. "What are you *talking* about?"

"Quit it, Orly," Corrie told him. "Meredith's from Calgary. She doesn't know that game." She explained to Meredith how every time you saw a monkey puzzle tree you were supposed to pinch someone and say what Orly had said. Then the other person wasn't allowed to pinch back.

"They're sure weird-looking trees," said Meredith as they continued down the steep street. She looked around carefully until she saw another tree with long prickly branches that looked like monkeys' tails. Then she caught up to Orly. "Monkey tree! No pinchies back!"

Orly giggled and ran ahead to the house.

"We're here," said Corrie shyly.

"What a *huge* hedge!" said Meredith. They pushed open the sagging gate. Juliet and Orly dashed around to the back to bury the robin.

"Wow," said Meredith. "Your house is *enormous*! Your family must be *rich*!"

Corrie was confused. "I don't think we're rich. This used to be my grandparents' house. After they died, my parents moved into it."

Meredith gaped at the tall grey house. All the lower windows were obscured by overgrown shrubs. "How many rooms are there?"

Corrie shrugged. "Lots." She led Meredith up the mossy steps, through the hall, and into the dining room and kitchen. If only there were chocolate chip cookies warm from the oven waiting on the table!

The kitchen smelled sour. Mrs. Oliphant was reclining on the easy chair she'd dragged into the kitchen, smoking a cigarette and flipping through a movie magazine. She never baked cookies. "If you want something fancy you can make it yourself," she had told them.

She glared at Corrie. "Your younger brother has been driving me crazy," she said. "He comes down every hour asking for something to eat. I'm only here to cook and clean, not take care of sick children. And that damned cat threw up furballs in the den. I refuse to put up with all this extra work. I'm going to speak to your father!"

Corrie ignored her. She grabbed a package of soda crackers, a knife, and a jar of peanut butter and hurried Meredith out of the kitchen and up the back stairs.

"Is that the *housekeeper*?" whispered Meredith, clutching the railing on the slippery stairs. Up and up they climbed, to Corrie's room on the third floor.

Corrie cleared a space on the rug and motioned Meredith to sit down. Her heart sank as Meredith noticed the spiderwebs on the ceiling, the peeling iron bedframe, the tattered eiderdown draped over the unmade bed, and Corrie's books and clothes mounded on the floor.

Meredith's room contained twin beds covered with pink counterpanes. Each bed had its own white nightstand. Her curtains were frilly white organdy and she had something called a "dressing table," with a pink skirt gathered around it. The material in the skirt matched the counterpanes.

If Corrie had known Meredith would be coming she would have tried to tidy up. None of the housekeepers had ever properly cleaned the bedrooms, and Mrs. Oliphant was the worst; she said there were too many stairs.

Meredith was staring at the far wall. "Is that something *growing*?"

"It's just a vine that came in through the top. The window won't close because it's warped," said Corrie, trying to sound nonchalant.

They leaned against the bed, nibbling crackers spread with peanut butter. "Your housekeeper isn't very *friendly*!" said Meredith. "What's her name?"

"Mrs. Oliphant. She only came a month ago. She's such a grouch! We call her the Elephant."

Meredith giggled. "Does the Elephant stay all day?"

"She shops for food for us and comes at ten, just before Fa goes to work."

"Does she eat with you?"

"No, she leaves us dinner in the warming oven."

"How many housekeepers have you had?"

Corrie thought a minute. "Five, I think. They all quit because the house is too big to clean. And before the twins started school, no one lasted long looking after them all day."

"Is the Elephant a good cook?"

"Terrible! Everything tastes the same. Aunt Madge was a good cook. She made great desserts, like gingerbread with lemon sauce, and chocolate pudding."

"Did your aunt live with you?"

Corrie hadn't meant to say anything about Aunt Madge. "Yes," she said quietly. "She came after ... after my mother died. But she only stayed for a year."

"Why did she leave? Didn't you *like* her?"

Corrie swallowed. "I liked her a lot. She was really nice to us. But ... well, her cousin was sick. So she went back to Winnipeg to look after her."

She could never say the other reason Aunt Madge had left. If only Meredith would stop asking so many questions!

Luckily Meredith was distracted by a large, shaggy grey cat sauntering into the room. "Oh, she's *beautiful*!" cried Meredith. "What's her name?"

"He ... Hamlet," said Corrie. She jumped up and buried her face in the cat's fur. "Hamlet because he's a pig!"

Hamlet *mrawwed* as Corrie dropped him heavily on Meredith's lap.

"You're so *lucky*! A dog would be better, but cats are almost as great. Oh, I *wish* my father wasn't allergic to animals! Is Hamlet *yours*?"

"He's supposed to belong to all of us, but he likes Harry best." Corrie watched Meredith tickle Hamlet's ears. Hope flickered in her. Meredith was snoopy, but it was fun having her sitting here. Corrie hadn't had a friend in her room since she was eight.

"What a funny name he has," said Meredith, rolling Hamlet onto his back and stroking his stomach. Hamlet purred like a well-stoked engine.

"He's named after a play by Shakespeare. We all are." Now Corrie actually felt like telling Meredith more about her family.

"You are? I don't know a *thing* about Shakespeare," confessed Meredith.

"I don't know much. But I know the names of all the plays our names are from."

"Corrie is in a play? That's neat!"

"Cordelia. That's my real name. It's from *King Lear*. Sebastian is from *Twelfth Night*, Roz is Rosalind in *As You Like It*, Harry is from *Henry IV*, Orly is Orlando from *As You Like It*, and Juliet is from *Romeo and Juliet*."

"'Cordelia' is *much* more interesting than 'Meredith.'"

"'Meredith' is more normal. We all envy Harry—he got the most ordinary name."

As if on cue, Harry wandered in.

"This is Meredith," Corrie told him, wishing he didn't look so solemn.

Harry nodded at Meredith, squatted on the rug, and started wolfing down crackers as fast as he could spread them with peanut butter.

"Are you feeling better?" Corrie asked him.

Harry wiped his nose on a sleeve that was already encrusted with mucus. "A bit. I'll go back to school tomorrow. The Elephant yells too much. My sea monkeys have hatched, Corrie. Want to see them?"

They went into Harry's room and stared at dozens of tiny white dots swimming around in a jar. "They don't look at all like monkeys," said Corrie.

"Maybe they will when they get bigger," said Harry.

"*I* sent away for some of those," said Meredith. "My dad says they're just bugs."

They stared at the jar sadly. "What a gyp!" said Harry. "I spent all my allowance on them!"

"Never mind," said Meredith. "Maybe they'll grow into some weird kind of beetle or spider."

Harry gave her one of his rare smiles. He pulled out a large paper bag from under the bed. "Want to see my bottle-cap collection? I have two hundred and twenty-seven!" He started spreading them on the floor. "They're all numbered inside, see? I have a list."

"Do you want to tour the house?" Corrie asked quickly, before Harry could begin his endless bottle-cap litany.

First she showed Meredith the long narrow storage closet under the eaves that was packed with old suitcases and boxes. Meredith rummaged her way to the far end. Corrie nipped out and closed the door of Sebastian's room before she followed.

"This would be *perfect* for hide-and-seek!" said Meredith, pushing spiderwebs from her hair. "What's in all these boxes?"

"Fa's papers and stuff," said Corrie. She started to lead Meredith down the front stairs, but Meredith pointed to a door at the far end of the hall. "What's in *there*?"

Corrie swallowed. "Oh, just a spare room. We aren't allowed to go into it."

"Why *not*?" But Corrie was already halfway down to the second floor. She opened the door to Roz's room, first checking that Hamlet wasn't near. Meredith ran up to a cage by the window. "A *budgie*! What's his name?"

"Jingle." Corrie closed the door and opened Jingle's cage. She put in her hand and the green bird hopped onto her finger. Carefully she passed him to Meredith.

"He *tickles*! And he's so *tame*!" cried Meredith as Jingle hopped onto her shoulder and nuzzled her neck. "What a funny name you have," she told him.

"It's because of our last name—and because Roz got him for Christmas."

"Jingle *Bell*!" Meredith giggled as Jingle flew onto her head. "I wonder if Daddy's allergic to *birds*. I'm going to ask for one for Christmas! Does he *talk*?"

"Pretty boy!" said Jingle, as if he were waiting for her to ask. "Pretty Jingle! Merry Christmas! Merry Jingle Bell!"

Meredith was enthralled. Finally they returned Jingle to his cage and inspected Juliet and Orly's chaotic, smelly cave.

"Whose room is *that* one?" asked Meredith, pointing to a closed door across from the twins' room. "Your dad's?"

Corrie gulped. "It was, when my mother was alive. Now Fa sleeps in his study. Then he can get up and work in the middle of the night if he wants to."

Meredith kept staring at the closed door. "Can't we see in there?"

"No!" said Corrie. Then she added, "Sorry," but Meredith didn't seem to mind.

She took Meredith into Aunt Madge's old room. They stood a moment at the window. Below them, the twins were huddled together. Aunt Madge had left her white china dogs on either side of the mantel. Even after two years, Corrie could smell 4711 cologne in the air.

They went down the wide staircase and paused on the landing. "When it's sunny, the windows make rainbows on the walls," Corrie explained.

"*Really*? How?"

"Because of the bevels in the glass."

"Cool! Maybe I could come back and *see* that sometime."

"Um ... maybe you could. Come on, I'll race you down the stairs."

Corrie quickly showed Meredith the dark living room and, beside it, the large cluttered den, crammed with bookcases and squashy chairs and the TV. "We never use the living room—this is where we spend most of our time," she told Meredith. They glanced at the dining room and pantry, and Corrie pointed out the closed door that was Fa's study.

"Why do you call your father Fa and not Dad or Daddy?" Meredith asked.

Corrie shrugged. "I don't know—we always have. It's short for Father, I guess." She smiled at the idea of calling her father Daddy; it would be like calling a lion a kitten.

"Where is he?"

"He's at the university—he gets home about six. Want to see the basement? It's pretty spooky."

"I *like* spooky!" said Meredith. They crept down the stairs and along a dark passage to rooms stuffed with boxes, baby furniture, old bikes, and tools.

"You could get *lost* in this house!" said Meredith as they returned to the front hall.

"When we first moved here I did," Corrie told her. "I was only three and my legs got tired from climbing all the stairs."

"It's so *mysterious*!" said Meredith, gazing at the dark wood panelling. "There are so many hidden things, like the back staircase and the secret cupboard and all those closed doors. And *four* bathrooms! I've never heard of a house with four bathrooms. You are *so* lucky, Corrie. This is like a house in a book!"

The last of Corrie's reserve melted. Meredith didn't seem to mind the peeling wallpaper or the dust or the musty smell or the general mess. She was brave enough to explore the scary basement. She didn't even think Corrie was strange for not having a mother. She seemed to like her just the way she was.

Meredith looked out the window. "It's stopped raining—can we go in the back yard?"

They found Juliet and Orly standing solemnly in front of a rock in the garden. Their arms were black to their elbows and their faces were smudged with dirt.

Other rocks dotted the space. "This is our animal graveyard," Juliet told Meredith. "So far we have three birds, six turtles, and one rat."

"A *rat*! I'm scared of rats!"

"So am I," said Corrie, shivering at the memory of the ones Hamlet had killed. But she was glad Meredith was afraid of them too.

Juliet looked at both of them scornfully. "Me and Orly aren't afraid of rats!"

"You just missed the robin's funeral," said Orly. "We sang 'All Things Bright and Beautiful.'"

Corrie showed Meredith her favourite cherry tree. She suggested climbing it, but Meredith told her she was afraid of heights. The rest of the yard was a tangle of shrubs, trees, and uncut grass. Corrie thought of Meredith's pristine back lawn, where she and Meredith had practised cartwheels.

But Meredith seemed to like the wildness. "It's like a *jungle!*" she said, pushing through a thick clump of bamboo.

The yard was long and narrow. Corrie followed Meredith to the back. "What's *that?*" asked Meredith, pointing to a ramshackle cedar shed beside the gate to the lane.

"Oh, nothing," said Corrie quickly. "Just an old shed with ... with garden tools in it."

"Can I peek?" Meredith approached the grimy window, but Corrie pulled at her sleeve.

"There's nothing to see. Come on, let's go back to my room." She led Meredith back into the house.

Upstairs, Meredith bent over Corrie's desk. "What's *this?*"

"It's called a diorama," said Corrie shyly. Meredith peeked into the scene Corrie had created in a shoebox.

"How did you *do* it?"

"I used a mirror for the pond and some of Jingle's gravel for the sand. I drew the tree and barn on cardboard and then I cut them out and glued them on with little tabs so they'd stand up. It's not quite finished—I'm going to borrow some of the twins' wooden farm animals if I can sneak them out of their room."

"It's *wonderful!*"

Corrie glowed. "I've made lots of them," she said. "There's no room in here, so I keep them in the basement. I'll show you sometime."

"I'd *love* to see them!" Meredith sat on the bed and began to tell Corrie all about her house in Calgary and her best friends there. "I miss them *so* much. This school is kind of unfriendly compared to my other one. But at least *you're* nice to me, Corrie. When's your birthday?"

"August twentieth," said Corrie.

Meredith squealed. "So's *mine*! Isn't that *amazing*? We're twins! I *knew* we had lots in common the moment I met you!"

Corrie was enjoying Meredith so much that she forgot to listen for the front door to open. When it did, her heart leapt: Sebastian was home! What would he think about her new friend?

"Do you want to meet my brother and sister?" she asked, trying to sound casual.

"Sure!" said Meredith. "What's that noise?"

Corrie laughed. "Come and see!"

They ran down to the landing in time to see Orly slide down the banister and squeal as he hit the newel post at each level. Juliet and Harry waited behind to take their turn.

"Sebastian, Sebastian!" all three chanted. Corrie and Meredith picked their way through the tangle of arms and legs at the bottom of the stairs.

A tall boy and a shorter girl stood in the hall. Roz was scolding the twins. "Stop pawing at me—your hands are filthy!"

All the way down Corrie had looked forward to introducing Sebastian to Meredith. But when she saw his face, her good spirits vanished. Sebastian was miserable—pale and tense, his mouth quivering.

"Who's your friend, Corrie?" asked Roz.

Corrie had almost forgotten her. "Oh, this is Meredith. Meredith, this is Roz and ... Sebastian." Corrie kept examining him. He caught her eye and managed a small smile. Then he went into the hall bathroom.

"What happened?" Corrie asked Roz.

"The same as usual," sighed Roz. "I'll tell you later. Is Meredith staying for dinner?"

"She has to go home," said Corrie.

"But I'd *love* to stay!" said Meredith. "I'll phone my mum and ask her."

"We don't have enough food for you to stay," said Corrie.

"Corrie, don't be so rude!" said Roz.

Sebastian came out of the bathroom and started up the stairs. Roz grabbed each twin by the arm. "Come on, you two. Let's get you washed."

"Let go!" they screamed. Orly twisted his hand out of Roz's, and Juliet growled like a terrier.

Sebastian looked down from the landing. "Master Jules and Master Orlando, do as you are told," he said quietly.

"Yes, sire," they chorused, following Roz into the bathroom.

"*What* did they say?" asked Meredith. "'Yes, *sire*'?"

"It's just a silly game the twins play. Meredith, *please* go home. I need to be alone with my family, okay?"

Looking hurt and puzzled, Meredith put on her jacket and opened the door. She called back, "Goodbye, Corrie. I had a *really* good time."

Corrie barely heard her. She had already started up the stairs to talk to Roz.

2

The Round Table

"Terry pushed his head into the toilet," said Roz, cradling Jingle against her chest and stroking his head with her fingertip.

"Into the *toilet*? That's horrible!" Corrie pulled Roz's yellow chenille bedspread around her and leaned against the wall. "What did Sebastian do to make Terry so mad?"

Roz shrugged. "Nothing, probably. He's just out to get him, the way he was all last year. And he's got all his friends after Seb too. They follow him down the hall whispering names."

"What names?"

"'Homo' and 'Sebastian Bastard.'" Roz's round blue eyes looked hopeless.

She's so pretty, Corrie thought. But Roz looked too grown up. Her best friend, Joyce, had given her a perm, and now stiff blond waves framed her face. She was wearing a crisp white blouse tucked into a full skirt that showed off her tiny waist. On her cardigan she wore a pin that said "I Love Elvis." Roz and Joyce had gone to the Elvis concert the month before. They couldn't see or hear a thing, but ever since then Roz had been obsessed with him.

Roz sighed. "If only Sebastian would cut his hair! If he didn't look so different they might leave him alone."

"I *like* his hair!" said Corrie. "He's fine the way he is! He's different because he's better than all those other boys! They're thugs!"

"Of course he's better," said Roz, "but if he doesn't want to be bullied he could give in a bit. This whole family is different! I'm tired of it. Last year Joyce and I were too scared to join anything, but now that we're in grade eight we've made a pact. By the end of this term we're going to be popular. We read an article in *Seventeen* that tells you how. We have to act confident and join things. So we've tried out for baton and Glee Club. I really, really want to get on the baton team. But it doesn't help when everybody thinks your brother is such a loser!"

Corrie wanted to hit her. Instead she shook her arm; Jingle squawked and flew up to the curtains. "Sebastian's *not* a loser! How can you say that? It's only Terry and those other guys who think he is. You know that, Roz! Are you going to turn against Sebastian too?"

"Sorry, Corrie," said Roz. "I know he's not a loser. He's just Sebastian. I'll never turn against him. It's just hard sometimes, that's all." Jingle landed on the bedspread and marched up and down, picking at the tufts.

"I don't see why you care so much what other people think," said Corrie. "*I* don't. I like our family just the way it is."

"Wait until you get to junior high, then you'll care," said Roz. "It's so important how you look and act. If you're the least bit unusual you won't have any friends."

"Who cares about friends? You have us!"

"*I* care," said Roz.

Sebastian pushed open the door.

"Seb, I've told you to always knock!" said Roz. "Jingle's loose!" She cornered the budgie, snatched him up, and put him in his cage.

"Sorry," said Sebastian. "I just wanted to tell you we're having a meeting."

"Now?" said Roz. "It'll be so cold out there, and we haven't set the table yet."

"It's only five," said Sebastian. "The Elephant has just left and there's lots of time before Fa gets home. Can you get the others and meet me at Camelot?"

His grey eyes pleaded. Silently Roz and Corrie got off the bed and followed Sebastian down the stairs.

THE AIR IN THE SHED was so chilly they had to wear their winter jackets. Corrie pulled hers down to protect her bottom against the damp wood. Her stool was an uncomfortable stump. She helped Juliet pull hers closer into the circle.

Sebastian waited until everyone was seated and quiet around the Round Table. Then he spoke.

"I, Sir Lancelot du Lac, in the absence of our king, call a meeting of the Knights of the Round Table. Pray answer as I call your names. Sir Gawain."

"Present, sire," said Roz.

"Master Cor, my squire."

"Present, sire," said Corrie proudly.

"Master Harry, Sir Gawain's squire."

Harry blew his nose, then croaked, "Present, sire."

"Sir Gawain's page, Master Orlando."

"Present, sire!" squealed Orly.

"My page, Master Jules."

"Present," said Juliet.

"Present, what?"

Juliet giggled. "Present, *sire.*"

Sebastian nodded. "Gramercy. I will now proceed to relate to my noble fellow knights and their servants what has befell me since last we met." He picked up *The Boy's King Arthur* and read to them how Sir Lancelot smote many knights in a tournament.

Corrie watched the colour return to Sebastian's pale cheeks as the tale went on. His face relaxed and his eyes lost their anxiety. She let her mind be partly at the tournament and partly in the chilly shed.

The walls were hung with painted shields made of garbage-pail lids, cardboard armour covered in tinfoil, and wooden swords. The Round Table used to be a scratched one in the basement. They had cut off its legs to make it low and painted it black. A neighbour had let them have the stumps after he had cleared his yard; they had lugged them home in Orly's wagon.

Sebastian had begun the Round Table game after Mum's death. Now it didn't seem like a game any more—gradually it had taken over almost every part of their lives. When they went grocery shopping with Fa, they were riding on horseback to a fair to select live pigeons and spices. Excursions to the beach were really boar-hunting expeditions. Even in school and church they were knights, squires, and pages. They would give knowing glances at one another, revelling in their secret identities.

Corrie listened to the adventures of her master, the "flower of all the knights." Nothing existed except the dim, safe space and Sir Lancelot's deep voice.

"And then he gat another great spear, and smote down twelve knights, and the most part of them never throve after." The story was over.

"That was swell!" said Orly. "I liked how you made the enemy knight's nose bleed."

"You were very, very brave, Sir Lancelot," said Juliet.

He smiled at her. "Gramercy, Master Jules. Now, have any of you any news to relate?"

Corrie took a deep breath. "I have no news, sire, but I have a request."

"What is it, my good squire?"

"Sire, I have been your squire for several years. Don't you ... do you not think it is time I was made a knight?"

Sebastian smiled. "I understand your desire, Master Cor. You have been a brave and faithful squire, and you would make an excellent knight. But if you became a knight I would no longer have a squire. And who would be *your* squire?"

Corrie chose her words carefully. "Sir Lancelot, perhaps Master Harry could squire you and me as well as Sir Gawain."

"That is an interesting idea, Master Cor. I will think upon it and let you know soon. But if you are to be knighted, you will have to pass a trial."

Corrie gulped. "I know that. I'll ... I will do anything you ask of me, Sir Lancelot."

"*I* want to be your squire!" said Orly.

"No, me!" said Juliet. "I'm tired of being a page."

Sebastian frowned. "Fie on thee, young pages! It will be many years before you are squires."

The twins looked rebellious, but they knew enough not to speak any further.

Roz glanced at her watch. "I beseech you, Sir Lancelot, to end this meeting soon so we can get ready for our evening feast."

"We will not be much longer. Are there any domestic affairs to discuss?"

Corrie remembered Miss Tuck's request. "Yes, sire. The pages are not washing. Their teacher has said they cannot enter the classroom unless their hands are clean."

"Cannot Sir Gawain remind them to wash?"

Roz scowled. "I do! But they ignore me."

"Is this correct, Master Orly and Master Jules?"

The twins squirmed under his stern gaze. "Yes, sire," they muttered.

"Listen to me. If you do not wash your hands and face every morning before school, you will be expelled from the Round Table. A knight is clean. If you want to be knights one day, you have to start behaving like them. Do you understand?"

They nodded solemnly. Orly had tears in his eyes.

Sir Lancelot became Sebastian. "It's serious," he said more gently, ruffling Orly's hair. "If your teacher is dissatisfied she'll tell Fa. Then he may think we need more supervision. The Elephant is awful, but at least she leaves us alone. You pages aren't babies. You're old enough to look after yourselves, the way the rest of us do."

Sebastian stood up and hoisted Juliet on his back. He bucked and reared like a horse, making her scream with laughter as they all scrambled out of the shed and went in to get ready for dinner.

It was corrie's turn to set the table. She carefully set out Fa's wine glass and milk glasses for the rest of them. She went into the kitchen, sniffing hungrily. Harry was scraping meat out of a cat-food tin while Hamlet complained loudly about how slow he was.

"What are we having?" Corrie asked Roz.

"Beans and wieners again," said Roz, opening the oven. "That woman is so lazy! I'm going to talk to Fa. He gives her money for meat. Why can't we have a roast or something?"

"Don't talk to him, Roz! If Fa thinks we're unhappy with the Elephant he might get rid of her."

"I'd *like* to get rid of her!" said Roz.

"But then we might get someone who bosses us around! And you know how Fa hates hearing about problems. We shouldn't bother him."

"Oh, all right," grumbled Roz. "Is that him?"

The front door opened. Orly ran into the hall and Corrie followed. "Hello, my dears," said Fa, kissing each of their foreheads. Orly wouldn't let go of his leg until Fa swung him high. "That's enough, now," he said. He took off his raincoat and shook it out. His fringe of grey hair and his heavy eyebrows were dripping. "Such a rain! I think I left my umbrella on the bus."

Corrie grinned. "That's the second one this month!" She ran to get Fa a towel. Then she called the others, helped Roz ladle beans over pieces of toast, and brought in the coleslaw Mrs. Oliphant had left in the fridge.

"Ah, beans on toast, my favourite!" Fa was smiling and rubbing his hands together. He seemed to have forgotten they had had the same meal three days ago. "Now, whose turn is it to say grace?"

"Forwhataboudooreceivedelordmakeus*trooly*thankful!" babbled Juliet.

"Is your cold better, Harry? Did you go to school?" Fa listened to Harry's answer. He smiled at Orly's description of the hamster and told Roz he'd brought home a library book for her project on Mexico.

Corrie watched him. She could never figure out if Fa was really interested in their lives. He always asked them questions and listened to them, but his voice was detached and polite. It was as if he were carefully playing the role of being a father.

But then, she supposed she was the same. Every day she prepared and saved up for dinner a story from school. Tonight she told Fa how Mr. Zelmach had taught them a new song instead of having arithmetic. "Our class is going to sing in a concert next year, Fa! For the centennial. In 1958, British Columbia will be one hundred years old!"

"Knowing how much you hate arithmetic, I imagine it was a relief for you to skip it, Cordelia." Corrie squirmed with pleasure. Of course Fa was interested in her! This hour with him was so precious. He had breakfast with them only if he got up in time, but he was always with the family for dinner.

Everyone tried to keep Fa content, to reassure him that they were getting along fine so he could do his work undisturbed. He was a lovely father, gentle and kind. Corrie could not remember him ever saying a cross word to her. But as she gazed at him she remembered Meredith telling her how her father had spent the whole of Saturday fixing her bike.

Fa probably didn't even know Corrie had a bike, and he certainly wouldn't know how to fix one. But Fa is the king! she reminded herself. He was King Arthur, far too busy running his kingdom to spend much time with his knights and their servants. That was why he had appointed Sir Lancelot to be in charge in his absence.

"And you, my boy?" Fa asked Sebastian. "Did you have a good day at school?"

Sebastian nodded, keeping his head bent over his plate. "We're going to start reading *A Midsummer Night's Dream* next week," he said quietly.

Sebastian always knew exactly the right thing to say. "Ah, that delicious morsel!" said Fa. "When you're done, I'll give you an article I wrote about Titania. Your teacher might be interested in seeing it. Do you know which edition you're reading?"

Sebastian shook his head. "I'll check and let you know tomorrow."

What would Fa think if he knew Sebastian had had his head thrust down a toilet?

Fa didn't used to be so removed. He had always been absent-minded, but when Mum was alive he was much more animated, often laughing and talking with her.

Every night after dinner the family had sat in the living room—in that large room that was now hardly ever used. Sometimes Fa would play "lion tamer" with Corrie and Harry. He would perch on a chair and growl. Corrie would announce his tricks to the rest of the family and Harry would crack an imaginary whip. Then Fa would chase them around the room and threaten to eat them. They would scream in mock terror and Mum would stop Fa, laughing so hard that tears shone on her cheeks.

Corrie swallowed the memory. Those uproarious scenes in the living room seemed like a play she'd once seen. Now the play was over forever.

WHILE SEBASTIAN AND HARRY did the dishes, Corrie made the next day's lunches. Fa had already kissed them each goodnight and retired to his study to work. Corrie knew that he was working on a book about *A Winter's Tale*, and that he also wrote many articles on Shakespeare for special journals. He often worked long into the night.

How could one writer be so important that someone could spend his whole life studying him? Perhaps she would find out when she was old enough to read Shakespeare's plays.

For now Corrie was happy to curl up in her window seat with *The Eagle of the Ninth*. But after a while she lowered the book and gazed out at the night sky. The rain had stopped and she could see a few stars. A half moon shone over the distant line of sea.

I love my room, thought Corrie. It wasn't pretty like Meredith's, but it felt as safe as a nest, high above the surrounding houses.

She sat there for a few more minutes, then she padded along the hall to Sebastian's room. She could hear the twins having a noisy bath downstairs; Sir Lancelot's sternness had obviously made an impression on them.

"Sebastian? May I come in?" He opened the door to her knock.

"Of course you may, Master Cor!" Corrie perched on the edge of the bed. The walls of Sebastian's tidy room were covered with meticulous drawings of knights: knights on horses, knights jousting, knights with falcons on their wrists. He was such a good artist, Corrie thought proudly.

"Do you really think you're ready to be knighted?" Sebastian asked Corrie, turning his desk chair around and leaning back in it.

"Yes, I do!"

Sebastian smiled. "Who would you like to be? Sir Perceval? Sir Lionel?"

"Sir Gareth." Corrie had read in her own copy of *A Boy's King Arthur* how Gareth had disguised himself as a kitchen boy when he first went to Camelot. Sir Kay mocked him and called him Beaumains because of his white hands, but Sir Lancelot defended him.

"Sir Gareth ..." Sebastian looked thoughtful. "That would suit you. Gareth is gentle and loyal. And he's Gawain's brother. There's only one thing ... didn't you read about how he dies?"

Corrie flushed. "Well, Sir Lancelot kills him. But it wasn't on purpose—he didn't recognize Sir Gareth."

She crossed her fingers as she waited for Sebastian to consider it. For weeks she had imagined herself as Sir Gareth. "We don't have to go that far in the story," said Sebastian finally. "Sir Gareth you will be."

Corrie tingled with pleasure. She wanted to keep on talking about becoming a knight, but she made herself change the subject.

"Um, Sebastian ..." she ventured. "Roz said Terry was mean to you again. She said that—"

"I don't want to talk about it," said Sebastian tightly. "That's school. It's not real."

Corrie flinched at the fierceness in his face, but she struggled on. "It's *quite* real, isn't it? I mean, you spend most of your day there."

"It was so much better when school was part of the Round Table—remember?"

Of course she remembered. When Sebastian and Roz had been at Duke of Connaught Elementary School, it had been a School for Knights. Art was Harping, Social Studies was Jousting, and Gym was Archery. Arithmetic, Corrie's most dreaded subject, had seemed much easier when she knew it was Falconry. Whenever she passed Sebastian or Roz or Harry in the hall they would exchange secret smiles, proud that they were really knights and squires heading for their next class in Hunting or Fencing.

But that had been more than two years ago. When Sebastian went to junior high, Corrie and Roz had tried to keep up the game, but it didn't work without Sir Lancelot's leadership. Now Corrie sometimes tried to be Master Cor at school, but with both of the knights gone it didn't gel for more than a few minutes.

Sebastian's eyes were as clear as grey glass. Corrie couldn't bear the anguish in them. "Couldn't you tell someone how cruel Terry is?" she asked him. "The principal, maybe?"

"You know I can't tell on him. That would make him go after me even more." Sebastian got up and looked out the window. "Nothing will work, Corrie. But it doesn't matter! I'm Sir Lancelot! This is nothing compared to killing two giants and smiting five knights with one spear! I can take it."

"Even when they stick your head—"

"Enough! I don't want to talk about it any more. Do you understand, Master Cor?"

Corrie bent her head. "Yes, sire."

"Now, about your knighthood. We could have your initiation and dubbing this Saturday. I will start thinking of a suitable trial."

"Corrie!" Roz was calling her from downstairs. "Would you please read to Juliet and Orly? I haven't done my homework yet."

The twins were rosy and pristine, each freshly washed head glistening. Meredith would love them like this: now they really did look like Freddie and Flossie.

They piled onto Juliet's bed and Corrie read them a chapter of *Henry Huggins*. Then she tried to kiss Juliet, but as usual Juliet growled and escaped under the covers.

Orly, however, loved to be cuddled. Corrie carried him to his own bed and savoured his clean smell while he clung to her. "Don't go yet," he begged. Orly was afraid of the dark.

"I'll leave the hall light on. You'll be all right," Corrie told him. She kissed him and handed him his favourite bear.

Corrie yawned as she brushed her teeth. This fall Sebastian had extended her bedtime to nine, but she wasn't used to the extra half-hour yet. She tried to read, but soon she had to turn out her light. She curled into her pillow and tried to clear out of her mind a vision of Sebastian's head being shoved into a toilet. Instead, she told herself a story about Sir Gareth slaying a dragon.

3

Sir Gareth

Saturday was the day the Bell family had the most freedom. Fa usually spent most of the day doing research in the university library. The Elephant didn't come on weekends. She left them groceries, and they had to concoct meals on their own.

Corrie woke up with her usual weekend elation—two whole days without school, two days just to sink into her family and not worry about the rest of the world. It was a perfect September morning, sunny and warm with a breath of wind.

School had been lonely that week. The day after Meredith had come to Corrie's house, she had rushed up as usual. Corrie had been so embarrassed at how rude she had been, however, that she turned her back and walked away. Meredith tried a few more times to talk to Corrie, then she gave up. Corrie couldn't bear the hurt, confused look on her face. She knew she should apologize, but it had been so long since she'd had a friend, she didn't know how.

But today she was to be made a knight! Last evening she had kept an hour's vigil in Camelot. Sebastian had lit candles for her and told her to ponder the Code of Chivalry, which was posted on the shed wall.

Corrie sat on her hard stump. The candle made scary flickering shadows. She tried to pretend she was in a chapel. She even tried to kneel, but the ground was so uncomfortable she gave that up after a few minutes.

I am twenty-one, thought Corrie, about to be knighted after seven years of service as a squire. Carefully she read aloud each line of the Code that Sebastian had painted in elaborate gold letters:

A knight is brave.
A knight never cries.
A knight is courteous.
A knight is generous and kind.
A knight is clean.
A knight protects the weak.
A knight fights evil and injustice.
A knight is noble.

"Do you think you can live up to all of it, Master Cor?" Sir Lancelot asked her when he came back.

"It will be hard to be so ... so perfect all the time," said Corrie.

Sir Lancelot looked solemn. "It *is* hard. Nobody expects you to be perfect, but you have to *try* to be perfect. That is what I do every moment."

She could never be like him. "I'll try," Corrie whispered. "But I'm not very strong."

Sir Lancelot patted her back. "You will be fine." He led her back to the house and she joined the others in front of the TV, feeling important as they gazed at her curiously.

"WE'LL DO THE TRIAL on the golf course," Sebastian announced at breakfast. He looked completely relaxed—Corrie knew he relished weekends even more than she did.

Hamlet was on the table, dipping his paw in Harry's cereal. Roz picked him up and dropped him on the floor. "I'm not coming," she told them.

Sebastian frowned. "Not coming, Sir Gawain? Not coming to the initiation and dubbing of Sir Gareth?"

"I'm sorry, Corrie. I know it's an important occasion. But Joyce and I have to practise baton for the tryouts next week."

"Baton!" Sebastian looked disgusted. "This is much more important than a stupid girls' thing."

Roz stood up. "It's not stupid to *me*. You'll just have to do without me. I'll be back about five to get dinner ready." She flounced out of the kitchen.

"Why is Roz so mad all the time?" Orly asked.

Yes, why? thought Corrie. She watched Sebastian swallow his disappointment. He smiled at Orly and said, "Never mind, Master Orlando. Sir Gawain has gone on a quest. It is too bad, but it is unavoidable. Now, my men, get your arms and let us go!"

They left the dishes and ran out to Camelot to collect their things. Everyone had wooden swords, even the pages. Sebastian said that, properly, they wouldn't have, but Juliet and Orly had made such a fuss that he had made them little ones. Corrie thrust her own sword carefully through her belt. Its paint was wearing off and the handle was loose; she'd have to fix it later.

Sir Lancelot's sword was the largest; it even had a name, Joyeux. He also had a large shield painted with three scarlet stripes, symbolizing that he had the strength of three men.

But Sebastian hadn't been able to wear his arms in public since he'd started junior high—it was too great a risk. Someone from his school might see him. He glanced at his sword and shield and armour longingly as the others got ready.

Corrie straightened her sword as they trotted their horses down the steep sidewalk. Was she getting too old to ride her horse in public as well? She wondered how she would feel if she passed a classmate, and decided she wouldn't care.

The horses—"palfreys," as Sir Lancelot called them—were long pieces of bamboo they had cut from the back yard. Each had reins braided with small bells. Corrie's used to be Midnight, but today she was changing his name. Sebastian had looked in all his books, but he couldn't find a name for Sir Gareth's palfrey. Corrie decided to call him Lightning.

Lightning was chestnut with a white streak down his forehead. He had a long mane and was so wild that only Corrie could ride him. She pulled back on the reins to stop Lightning's eager lunging.

Sebastian strolled nonchalantly behind them, as if he were babysitting his younger brothers and sisters. But Corrie knew he was really dressed in full armour and mounted on his noble black steed, on the lookout for any evil knights or giants they might encounter.

Sebastian was carrying lances, an armful of bows and arrows, and a brown paper bag. Corrie quaked when she noticed the bag: she knew it had something to do with her trial. But this morning she felt invincible, certain she could pass whatever trial Sir Lancelot had in mind for her.

The golf course at the end of their street had not been used for years. Now it was a huge, glorious playground. For most of her life Corrie had played there. Graceful weeping willow trees dotted the green space, and the neighbourhood kids made forts and hideouts in the high bushes along the fence.

Master Cor galloped Lightning over the rough grass, racing Master Harry and winning. They reached a clearing in a dense grove of trees. This was Joyous Gard, Sir Lancelot's castle. Sometimes other kids were here and they had to go to another part of the golf course, but today the clearing was empty. They could be private for the trial.

"Dismount from your steeds," ordered Sir Lancelot. They lined up the bamboo sticks along the lower limbs of a tree. "Come here, Master Cor."

Corrie stood in front of Sir Lancelot, and all her confidence vanished. What if the trial were too hard? She couldn't bear to let him down.

"Master Cor, what is the first article of the Knight's Code?"

"A knight is brave."

"Correct. Every knight must be brave. Thus your trial must involve doing something that you are afraid to do. I know that you have a great fear of rats, do you not, Master Cor?"

Not *rats*! But Corrie made herself whisper, "Yes, sire."

Sir Lancelot picked up the paper bag. "If a knight is afraid of a harmless creature like a rat, what will he do if he encounters a dragon or a griffin? Yesterday I found another dead rat that the castle cat killed. It is in this bag. This is your trial, Master Cor. You are to take the rat out of the bag, put it on that rock, and sit beside it without removing your gaze from it for fifteen minutes. If you can do that, you will be brave enough to be knighted."

I can't! Corrie cried inside. Her heart pounded and her mouth felt parched. She couldn't bear rats at a distance—how could she look one in the eye? How could she *touch* it?

For a few minutes she couldn't speak. Sir Lancelot said gently, "Remember that the rat is dead, Master Cor. It cannot hurt you. Remember that in fifteen minutes your trial will be over forever."

Corrie swallowed. *A knight is brave.* She pictured Sir Lancelot and Sir Gawain calling her Sir Gareth and the squire and pages calling her sire. Sir Lancelot would carve "Gareth" into her wooden stool; maybe she'd even get her own shield.

This was the hardest thing she'd ever done in her life. Her only choice was to force herself to do it.

"All right," she muttered. "I'm ready."

"Good for you." Sir Lancelot handed her the bag. Before Corrie had time to think about it, she put in her hand and grasped a pinch of damp fur.

"Ewww, it stinks!" squealed Master Jules.

"Quiet!" ordered Sir Lancelot.

Corrie held the rat as far away from her as she could and walked over to the rock. The rat was limp and heavy, like a little sack of stones. She draped it over the rock and closed her eyes.

"Open your eyes, Master Cor. Sit beside the rat and keep looking at it. The rest of you stand over here without a word."

Corrie sat on the grass and clutched her trembling knees. She stared at the rat. It was a large one with a long pink naked tail. Its dark fur looked greasy. Its beady eyes were still open and stared malevolently up at her. A rank odour rose from it. Worst of all was its long nose extending over its horrible little mouth.

Corrie's heart thudded so hard it hurt her chest. She thought she would choke. At first she could hear distant traffic, the call of a gull, and Harry blowing his nose. Then she felt herself fading, as if she were shrinking into her body.

She kept her eyes on the rat but she no longer saw it. Instead she saw a black box. She was sitting in a hot, crowded church, leaning against Fa. The air smelled like lilies. Mum was in the black box; that's what the grown-ups said. Eight-year-old Corrie kept staring at it. She glanced at Fa's face. He was staring at the box too, and his face was so rigid that Corrie felt even more scared.

Corrie started to sway. Immediately Sebastian's hands were on her shoulders. "Corrie? Are you all right?"

Corrie came back. She looked up at Sebastian's concerned eyes. "Is the time up?" she whispered.

"Not quite, but you've done long enough. Are you sure you're all right? Maybe I picked too hard a trial."

It was so comforting to feel Sebastian's hands on her shoulders that Corrie leaned back against him for a few seconds. She took a deep breath and then she realized her trial was over.

She jumped to her feet, turning her back on the rat. "I'm fine! I did it! Now would you *please* get rid of that rat?"

Sebastian looked relieved. "Well done, Master Cor! Master Orlando, you may dispose of the rat."

"Yes, sire!" Orly rushed over and picked up the rat by the tail, swinging it around his head several times before he threw it into the bushes. Juliet and Harry cheered.

"Were you really scared, Corrie?" Juliet asked her. "*I* wouldn't have been!"

"Everyone is afraid of different things, Master Jules," said Sir Lancelot. "Master Cor has passed his trial. Master Harry, please dress your knight in his new vestments."

Solemnly Harry drew out armour and a sword and shield from another paper bag. Corrie hadn't even noticed him carrying it. Harry tied pieces of tinfoil-covered cardboard onto her upper arms. He unfastened her old sword and fixed the new one to her belt.

The new sword was flat wood sharpened to a point, painted silver. The crossguard was made of cardboard with tinfoil glued on it; above it the handle was wrapped with black tape, and on top was a black pommel made out of a drawer handle. The shield was even more splendid, painted with a coat of arms: brown acorns, a black dog's head, and a yellow star. Sebastian must have been working on them all week.

"They're beautiful!" said Corrie. "What do the symbols mean?"

"The acorns mean strength, the dog means loyalty, and the star means you are a noble person. These are all qualities you have shown as a squire, Master Cor, and I know you will continue to show as a knight."

Corrie could hardly breathe for pleasure. Sir Lancelot directed her to kneel in front of him. "I now dub thee Sir Gareth, noble knight of King Arthur's Round Table," said Sir Lancelot, tapping a sword on each of Corrie's shoulders. "Arise, Sir Gareth."

Corrie stood up slowly. Orly hugged her while Juliet and Harry pounded her on the back. "Congratulations!" they all cried.

Sebastian beamed. "Congratulations from me also, Sir Gareth. I look forward to the two of us having many adventures together."

"Thank you," whispered Corrie. She was a real knight!

"*Hi*, Corrie!"

They turned around quickly. Meredith! She was standing there with her bike. "I didn't expect to see *you* here, Corrie! I was exploring this old golf course, except it's too bumpy to ride on." She gazed curiously at the weapons strewn on the ground. "What are you *doing*?"

Corrie flushed. "Hi, Meredith," she muttered. "We're ... we're just playing a game."

"Can I play too?"

"No!" Sebastian glared at Meredith as if she were an enemy. "It's a private game."

Meredith turned her bike and walked it away quickly. But Corrie had seen the tears spring to her eyes.

"*Why* can't she play?" she said, surprised at her boldness. "We need another squire. She'd probably be happy to be mine."

Corrie refused to lower her eyes as Sebastian stared at her.

"Sir Gareth, I am shocked," he said tersely. "You know the Round Table is just for us. No one from outside has ever belonged to it."

"Why not?" repeated Corrie stubbornly. Being a knight gave her courage.

"Because ..." Sebastian looked desperate. "Because it's just not *right*, that's why. Because then it wouldn't be a secret any more. It wouldn't be special, it wouldn't be ... safe!"

Safe? Corrie watched Sebastian's face. The haunted look he had each day when he arrived home from school was there again—the fear.

"I'm sorry," she whispered. "It's all right, Sebastian. Meredith doesn't have to be one of us. I won't ask again."

Sebastian smiled tightly. "Thank you, Sir Gareth. I accept your apology. We will forget about it. Now, let us see how you fare in a sword fight against Master Harry!"

Corrie tried to be Sir Gareth again as she pinned Harry against a tree with her sword. Then Sir Gareth and Sir Lancelot charged each other with lances, trying to knock each other down. "Will you submit?" Sir Lancelot asked as Sir Gareth fell off his palfrey to the ground.

"I submit!" she cried, trying not to laugh.

They had archery practice, then they galloped up and down chasing imaginary deer. Finally they trotted back to the house for lunch. But all the way Corrie kept looking out for Meredith.

The rest of the day was so pleasant that Corrie tried to forget about her confrontation with Sebastian. Roz came home extremely cheerful. She congratulated Corrie on becoming a knight and cooked them delicious sausages for dinner.

Fa always watched TV with them on Saturday nights. They were pleased to discover that *Hamlet* was on because they knew how much he would enjoy it. Corrie didn't understand much of the movie, but that meant she could ask a lot of questions and get Fa's full attention as he patiently answered them.

"Look, Hamlet, it's all about you!" said Harry. He had found an old golf ball that afternoon. He'd peeled off the cover and was laboriously unwinding the long rubber strand underneath. When he reached the tiny black ball in the middle he threw it for Hamlet, who trotted back with it as if he were a dog. Then Hamlet dozed in Harry's lap. The twins fell asleep as well, and Fa helped carry them to bed.

EVERY SUNDAY MORNING, rain or shine, the Bell family walked five blocks to St. George's Church. If it rained they arrived like a flock of wet sheep, shaking the water off their coats and shoes.

Corrie often wished they had a car, but Fa had sold theirs soon after the accident. *Accident* ... that word had hovered in the air like a black cloud the evening Fa had come home late, stood in the hall with a white, stricken face, and whispered, "My dears, there's been an accident."

Fa had been driving when a truck hit Mum's side of the car and killed her instantly. It wasn't his fault—the grown-ups kept saying that over and over. But he thought it was, and he swore that he would never drive again.

Poor, dear Fa, thought Corrie, walking behind her father as he strode into the church, a twin in each hand. She enjoyed the way people stared at them, this large family led by such a distinguished-looking father.

They took up a whole pew. Corrie smoothed her dress over her knees and adjusted her beret; Roz always made them dress up for church. And they looked nice, Corrie thought. Yes, Orly's knees beneath his short pants were scabbed, and Juliet's pink dress, handed down from Corrie, was too long for her. Harry's shirt was wrinkled, and her own sweater had holes in the sleeves. But Fa wore the tweed jacket and matching waistcoat he did every Sunday, and Roz, of course, was a model of teenaged elegance. Sebastian wasn't dressed much differently from every day but he always looked meticulous, with his gleaming dark, chin-length hair and his serious grey eyes.

To Corrie's delight the first hymn was "To Be a Pilgrim," Sebastian's favourite. She grinned at him as they shared a hymn book and their voices rang out together: "No foe may still his might, though he with giants fight." They were Sir Lancelot and Sir Gareth, attending chapel before a battle.

As Corrie put down her hymn book, she spotted a curly dark head under a red hat a few pews away: Meredith! She'd never seen her in church before.

A few minutes later all the children paraded out for Sunday school. Meredith avoided Corrie's eyes. She must have really been hurt yesterday.

Corrie sat around a table with the rest of the ten- and eleven-year-olds. She paid no attention to Mrs. Rose, the Sunday school teacher, who was reading them the story of Jonah and the whale. Instead she pondered how she could make amends with Meredith.

Finally she excused herself to go to the bathroom. With relief, she heard Meredith make the same request. Outside the door they gazed at each other awkwardly.

"I didn't know you went to this church," mumbled Corrie.

"This is our first Sunday."

"I'm really sorry about yesterday," Corrie continued quickly. "Sebastian's like that sometimes, but I *wanted* you to play with us."

"You did?" Meredith's face was hopeful but wary. "I'd *like* to be friends with you, Corrie, but this week you've been so unfriendly I decided you didn't."

"I do!" Corrie cried. "It's just … it's just hard with my family, that's all."

"I *like* your family! They're kind of strange, but they're *interesting*. Can you come over to my house tomorrow after school?"

"Sure!" They grinned at each other.

"Was that your *father* sitting with you?" Meredith asked.

Corrie nodded.

"He's so *old*!"

"I guess he *is* old for a father. He's—uh, he was—twenty years older than my mother."

"You're It!" cried Meredith, tapping her on the shoulder. Corrie chased her all over the parish hall. They played tag until Sunday school was over, then they joined the line of children to meet their parents coming out of church. Mrs. Rose frowned at them, but there was nothing she could do. Sunday school teachers had no authority, not like the ones in real school.

THE REST OF SUNDAY was as peaceful as usual. The family squished into a taxi and Fa took them downtown for lunch, to the hotel restaurant they went to every week. No one there seemed to mind the twins getting up and down, running into the lobby, and coming back to report on what they'd seen.

This was the only good meal they had all week. Corrie stuffed herself with roast beef and Yorkshire pudding and apple pie with thick cream. Fa and Sebastian were engaged in a lively conversation about the Holy Grail; Fa knew a lot about knights, almost as much as Sebastian.

Corrie wondered if he guessed he was King Arthur. He must have noticed their game. But maybe not; Fa was so immersed in his own secret world, he was barely aware of much outside it.

But at least on Sundays he stayed out of his study and tried to give all his attention to his children. After the taxi ride home, they changed their clothes and went for a long walk on the golf course. Then they all sat in the den with ginger ale for them and wine for Fa.

Corrie and Harry stretched out on the floor with the weekend funnies. Harry's favourites were "Terry and the Pirates" and "Mark Trail"; Corrie liked "Gasoline Alley" and "Prince Valiant." Prince Valiant looked so much like Sebastian, with his long hair and handsome demeanour. And he was just as brave. Hamlet plopped down on top of the paper the way he always did when someone read on the floor.

Fa played cribbage with Roz, Orly curled up in his lap. "When did your hair get so curly, Rosalind?" Fa asked suddenly.

Roz looked irritated. "Oh, Fa, I got a perm three weeks ago! Don't you remember? I asked you if I could."

Fa looked ashamed. "I do apologize, my dear. I forgot." He studied her. "It makes you look much older. You're getting to be quite a young lady!" He looked surprised that any of them were growing at all.

Fa admired Harry's model airplane and tried unsuccessfully to teach Juliet how to tie her shoelaces, laughing with the rest of them when Juliet simply knotted the two loops. "It's my *invention*," she boasted. "Fa, could Orly and me get some more turtles?"

"Orly and *I*," said Fa. "I thought you already had turtles."

"They died," said Juliet.

"They *always* die," said Roz. "I don't think you should buy any more."

Juliet looked so woeful that Fa said they could ask for turtles for Christmas.

"Fa," said Harry solemnly, "a kid in my class says that if you cut the skin between your thumb and first finger you'll die. That couldn't be true, right?"

Fa smiled. "We thought that when *I* was young! No, it's not true. It's just a superstition."

"What's a stition?" asked Orly.

"A superstition is something that is untrue but that many people believe is true," said Fa. "Like thinking that black cats are bad luck."

"They *are* bad luck!" said Orly. "I'm glad Hamlet is grey and not black."

Fa kissed the top of Orly's head. "You can think they are if you like."

Corrie watched Orly enviously; it didn't seem so long ago that she'd had that place on Fa's lap. She had to be content with leaning against his legs while she waited for a break in the chatter. Then she told Fa about reading *The Eagle of the Ninth* and asked him to tell her something about the Roman Empire. She had his whole attention for twenty minutes, and she learned a lot. Fa knew *everything*! He was better than an encyclopedia.

Then Fa asked them his usual weekly question: "Is everything all right, my dears? Are you managing with Mrs. Smith?"

"Mrs. Oliphant!" cried Juliet. "But we call her the Elephant!"

"Ah, yes, of course ... Mrs. Oliphant. I hope you don't call her that to her face, Juliet. You must never hurt people's feelings, you know. Is she doing a good job? Is she kind?"

Sebastian shot the others a warning glance. "Mrs. Oliphant is very nice to us. Everything's fine, Fa."

"I hope so," said Fa. "I don't want to overburden you. I can afford to hire Mrs. Elephant to stay longer in the evenings if you like." Juliet shrieked at his mistake, but Corrie knew that he'd said it on purpose.

"We really don't need her," Sebastian said. "We're fine in the evenings—right, Roz?" Roz looked as if she wanted to contradict him, but she didn't dare do anything but nod in agreement.

Corrie sighed. How could Fa not notice the dirty and untidy house and the awful meals? But he never did.

It was Sebastian's turn to cook Sunday supper. He made what he always did—hot dogs and carrot sticks. Harry sulked when Orly beat him in a hot-dog-eating contest: he ate three and a half to Orly's four.

After the meal they went back into the den and Fa read to them. He had a deep, rich voice, with a slight overlay of an English accent; he'd come to Canada from Devon when he was sixteen. Every Sunday in Corrie's life she had listened to him. What wonderful stories they had heard in this room! Lamb's *Tales from Shakespeare*, Grimms' *Household Tales*, *The Jungle Books* ...

Tonight Fa was reading *A Connecticut Yankee in King Arthur's Court*. Because there were knights in it, they all listened especially avidly. Corrie had managed to squeeze in beside Fa.

She stopped listening as a memory arose in her mind. She and Roz were sitting on each side of Aunt Madge on the same chesterfield, pushing into her and wailing like babies.

"You cry too, Sebastian," Aunt Madge had said, gazing with concern at eleven-year-old Sebastian standing by the fireplace. "Do try to, dear. It will help you feel better."

Sebastian had given Aunt Madge a look of utter scorn. "Don't tell me what to do! You're not my mother!"

Corrie had climbed onto Aunt Madge's lap and cried even harder.

The memory vanished when Orly clapped his hands to his mouth and dashed out of the room. Roz ran after him. When she came back a few minutes later with a pale-looking Orly, Harry said, "I won! Now I have more hot dogs inside me than you have!"

"I still ate more!"

"Now, boys," said Fa weakly. He looked at Sebastian. "Isn't it time for bed?"

4

A Quarrel

Corrie and Meredith sat in Meredith's bedroom, a plate of peanut butter cookies between them. Corrie leaned against two of the many stuffed dogs that crowded the bed.

"Tell me about your *game*," urged Meredith.

Corrie flushed. "Well," she began slowly, "we're all knights of the Round Table. Sebastian is Sir Lancelot, the bravest knight—he's our leader. We pretend Fa is King Arthur, who's always away on a quest. And sometimes he's Merlin, because he knows so much. Roz is Sir Gawain, and now I'm Sir Gareth. That's what we were doing on the golf course—I had just been dubbed. Harry's the squire for all the knights, and Juliet and Orly are our pages."

"Cool!" said Meredith. She didn't seem to think any of this was too weird. "I know all about knights—I got a book about them for Christmas last year. But why are you all *men*?" she said. "Why isn't anyone Guinevere or Elaine?"

Corrie shrugged. "I don't know. I guess because knights have more adventures than ladies. Sometimes Guinevere is around, but she's imaginary. Lots of people have to be made up because there aren't enough of us."

"How long have you been playing this?"

"For a couple of years," said Corrie. "I was a page first, then Sebastian's squire. I groomed his horse and rode beside him in battle. Just pretending, of course," she added quickly.

Meredith nibbled on a cookie. "Sebastian really *seems* like a knight. I think I'm *afraid* of him!"

"You don't have to be. He was just surprised to see you on Saturday."

"Is he bossy in *real* life too? When you're not playing your game, I mean."

"He's not bossy! He's the nicest, kindest brother anyone could have!" Corrie tried to smile. "Maybe he *seems* bossy, but that's because he's our leader. He makes up our meal and bath sched-ules and gives out our allowances and tells us when to go to bed. We all help, of course. Roz buys our clothes, I make the lunches every day, and Harry and I take turns walking the twins home from school."

"But why doesn't your *father* do any of that?"

Too many questions! But now that Meredith was her friend, Corrie had to try to answer patiently. "Fa's always busy," she said. "He has very important work to do—he teaches classes and he's writing a book!"

"*That's* important," said Meredith solemnly. Then she giggled. "Why does Sebastian have such long hair? It makes him look like a *girl*!"

"He has to have long hair because Sir Lancelot had long hair— we have a picture. And I don't think he looks at all like a girl," Corrie added tightly.

"Sorry," said Meredith. "I don't *really* think he does. I think he's handsome. I *wish* Sebastian would let me play your game with you. I could be your *squire*!"

"I wish he would too."

"*I* know," said Meredith eagerly. "Why don't *we* pretend I'm your squire? Or I could be another knight! I could be Sir Perceval or Sir Galahad! You and I could go on quests and things, just like your family does. We'd be *secret* knights!"

"I don't think we should," Corrie said hastily. "I don't think Sebastian would like it."

"But he'd never *know*!"

"Maybe not, but I just don't want to, okay?"

Meredith shrugged. "Okay. Let's have a dog show, then."

Meredith had twenty-two stuffed animals. Corrie was especially intrigued by the tiny ones arranged in a circle on her chest of drawers: four bears, two raccoons, and a squirrel.

Nine dogs lived on the bed. It was fun to arrange them in groups for the judges, and to make awards out of cardboard for the best-groomed, best-behaved, and best-looking dog. They were deep into the game when Meredith's mother knocked at the door.

"What do you think, girls?" she asked. On her head was perched a blue hat. A purple one was in her hand. "I'm trying to choose," she told them, coming in and sitting on the chair. "Which one do you like the best? The altar guild at St. George's is having a tea, and I want to make a good impression."

Mrs. Cooper would always make a good impression, thought Corrie. She was round like her daughter, but her face was so open and friendly. She wore bright lipstick and colourful clothes.

"Try on the other one," ordered Meredith, getting up and helping her mother adjust it. "No, I like the blue one best. What do *you* think, Corrie?"

"I like it best too," said Corrie shyly.

"The blue one it is, then! I'll take the other one back."

Meredith had crammed the purple hat on her head. She snatched the blue one from her mother's head and put it on Corrie's.

"Look how that hat brings out the colour in your eyes, Corrie," said Mrs. Cooper. "You're going to be very pretty when you grow up."

Corrie blushed. No one had ever said this to her before. She gazed at her face in the mirror, framed by the hat. Roz and Juliet were the pretty ones, not her. Her nose was too long and her face was so thin and freckled. She had never cared; knights didn't have to be pretty. But Mrs. Cooper was right. Beneath her long bangs her eyes looked bluer than usual.

"You have such shiny brown hair," Mrs. Cooper told her. "It would look lovely with the ends curled."

Corrie took off the hat and examined her bone-straight hair in the mirror.

"Would you like me to put it in pincurls for you?" Before Corrie could object, Mrs. Cooper had fetched a comb, some water, and a dish of bobby pins. Corrie sat in a chair while Mrs. Cooper deftly fastened strands of her hair into tight curlicues, crossing each round with two bobby pins. When she had finished, Corrie's head was a helmet of pins. They prickled, but she tried not to protest.

"There you go!" Mrs. Cooper patted her head. "It should be dry in about an hour, then I'll brush it out for you."

Corrie and Meredith went back to their dog show. "I hope you don't mind," said Meredith when her mother had left the room. "Mum likes playing with hair, and she can't do much with *mine* because it's already naturally curly."

"It's okay," Corrie told her, although she was afraid of what she would look like.

When the curls were all brushed out she examined herself warily.

"Wow!" said Meredith.

"You look gorgeous," said Mrs. Cooper.

Corrie was horrified. A stranger stared back at her, a fuzz of curls springing artificially from the ends of her hair. She looked like a teenager!

Mrs. Cooper hugged her. "Oh, sweetheart, you don't like it, do you? Don't worry, it'll be straight again in the morning. I'm sorry I did it. Do you forgive me?"

Corrie smiled. How could she not? She hated her hair, but it wouldn't last. It was almost worth going through the ordeal to get such a friendly hug.

"WHO CURLED YOUR HAIR?" Roz asked her in the kitchen. "I love it!"

"I don't," said Sebastian.

Corrie rushed to the sink and ran the cold-water tap. Gasping with the shock, she soaked her hair, then dried it on the dish towel. "There!" she said with relief. "All gone!"

"Oh, Corrie, why did you do that?" Roz shook her head. "You're such a tomboy!"

"Leave her alone, Roz," said Sebastian. "She's only eleven. She's much too young to curl her hair, and besides, knights don't care what their hair looks like."

"*You* do," said Roz bravely. "If you got yours cut you'd look more normal."

"My hair is my manhood," said Sir Lancelot. "If I cut it I will lose my courage. Pray do not ever suggest it again, Sir Gawain!"

He and Roz glared at each other. Lately the two of them had been more like a quarrelling brother and sister than fellow knights.

CORRIE STARTED GOING HOME with Meredith during lunch hour. At first she took her own carelessly made, dry sandwich with her. But the homemade soup, toasted sandwiches, puddings, and cookies that Mrs. Cooper offered her were so scrumptious that she started throwing away the sandwich. This was so much better than sitting in an almost empty classroom, a bored-looking teacher at the desk, with Harry and the twins and the few other kids who had to bring their lunch to school.

When it was Harry's turn to take home Juliet and Orly, Corrie spent the afternoon at Meredith's house. Soon she was sometimes staying for dinner on those days as well. Afterwards Mr. Cooper and Meredith would walk her home.

One Saturday morning at a Round Table meeting, Corrie was called to account for this. "Sir Gareth, you are eating too many meals at Meredith's house," Sir Lancelot told her. "It is not right. Her mother will think we are beggars."

"She doesn't mind," said Corrie. "She really likes cooking. Last night she made something called lasagna." Her mouth watered at the memory.

"This will not do," said Sir Lancelot sternly. "You and Sir Gawain are either away or late almost every night. I have to get dinner ready by myself, when we are supposed to be taking turns. I want this to stop immediately."

Roz looked furious. "That's not fair, Sebastian!" she cried. "You know I have baton two times a week, and other days I have drama and Glee Club. It's not any trouble to serve what the Elephant makes, and I always make dinners on Saturdays. And you don't have to wait for me—I can get something later."

"Sir Gawain, you are speaking out of turn. Kindly show more respect, and kindly address me by my proper name."

"I'll say what I want to, *Sebastian*," sneered Roz. "And I'll do what I want, too. School is really important to me right now. I'm not giving anything up!"

Sebastian glared at her. "The king does not like it," he said icily. "Last night he asked where you both were."

Roz's voice cracked, as if she were about to cry. "I'm sorry if Fa doesn't like it, but he'll have to get used to it. Things can't always stay the same, Seb."

She stood up, gave Sebastian a pleading look, and ran out of the shed.

The others sat there stunned. Orly edged closer to Corrie and took her hand. Corrie looked at Sebastian's stricken face. "I'm sorry, sire," she whispered. "If I'm home every night for dinner, can I still go for lunch? Mrs. Cooper really doesn't mind."

Sebastian smiled at her. "Thank you, Sir Gareth. That seems like a good compromise." Then he frowned. "I am wroth at Sir Gawain, who is acting strangely out of character. We will all send him to Coventry until he comes to his senses."

"Send him *where?*" asked Juliet.

"To Coventry. That means we will not speak to Sir Gawain all evening as a punishment," said Sir Lancelot.

"Not speak to *Roz?*" said Orly. He looked scared. "But what if she asks me something?"

"Do not answer," said Sir Lancelot grimly. He looked at their glum faces. "Let us forget this matter. Would you like to play Bestiary?"

"Yes!" said Juliet. She pulled out the bag of cards. Sebastian had invented the game last winter. He had drawn and labelled pictures of medieval beasts, then cut each card in half. They took turns drawing a half and placing it in the middle of the table. If a match came up, the first person to slap it and say "Beast!" got the pile. The game ended when one person ended up with all the cards.

"Beast!" cried Harry as he slapped a picture of a basilisk.

"Beast!"

"Ow, Orly, that was my hand!"

"Beast!"

"I said it first!"

"No, you didn't, I did!"

The playing became more and more boisterous as pictures of dipsas, manticores, griffins, and wethers were completed. The others were completely absorbed in the game, but Corrie couldn't pay attention and went out first.

She smiled at the racket but she felt sick to her stomach. She had never seen Sebastian and Roz quarrel like this. The Round Table had always been so harmonious: *A knight is courteous. A knight is generous and kind.*

Corrie had managed to placate Sebastian, but she was just as guilty as Roz. Ever since she'd become friends with Meredith she had neglected her family.

How could she do *anything* to bother Sebastian and Fa? Corrie resolved to be home every evening from then on.

SEBASTIAN WAS THE ONLY KNIGHT who managed to send Roz to Coventry. Corrie tried, but she was so torn by Roz's hurt expression that it lasted only a few minutes. The younger ones forgot immediately and chattered to Roz as usual.

"It's too hard for them," Corrie told Sebastian as they washed the dishes. "It's hard for me, too." She took a deep breath. "Anyway, I don't think it's right to ask us to punish Roz like that. *We* aren't mad at her."

She quivered inside. Would Sebastian send her to Coventry as well for defying him?

But he only looked tired. "I'm not angry with Roz any more. I just don't understand her! Sometimes she doesn't seem part of this family or the Round Table any more."

The Round Table *was* the family, Corrie thought. That made it doubly secure and safe—but also doubly hard to include anyone or anything outside it, like Meredith or baton.

She glanced at Sebastian's discouraged face. "How's school these days?" she asked carefully. "Are those boys still being mean to you?"

He lowered his head. "I do not wish to talk about school, Gareth. I have told you before, it is not real."

That meant he was still being bullied. If only she were really Sir Gareth and could smite Terry and his gang with her sword! But there was nothing she could do.

Sebastian tried to smile. "How's school for *you*, Corrie? Do you like your teacher?"

"Oh, yes! He's new. His name is Mr. Zelmach and he's really nice." She told Sebastian about how Mr. Zelmach didn't believe in homework.

"You're lucky," grimaced Sebastian. "I have tons of homework this year. I guess I'd better go upstairs and do it." He started out of the kitchen, but Corrie stopped him. She had thought of something to cheer him up.

"I have a request, Sir Lancelot. Could we not have a feast next weekend? We have not had one for a long time."

Sebastian's face relaxed. "An excellent idea, Gareth! A feast would do us all good. I praise your initiative for suggesting it. I will begin the preparations for it tomorn."

Roz continued to be edgy with Sebastian, but to Corrie's relief, she attended the feast. Sebastian gave Corrie money to buy potato chips, crackers and cheese, salami, and pop. Sir Lancelot told them they were eating wild boar, peacock, whale, swan, and rabbits. The squire and the pages carefully served each knight, then they helped themselves. They were allowed to eat with their hands.

"Sir Lancelot, tell us how you found the naked woman!" asked Orly.

"The one in the boiling water!" added Juliet.

"That was Elaine of Corbenic," said Sir Lancelot. After telling them the whole story he raised his glass of mead. "Let us drink a toast to the Round Table! May it last forever!"

"Forever!" they echoed. Corrie clinked her glass with Sir Gawain's, fervently wishing it could be true.

5

Sir Perceval

Mr. Zelmach was the best teacher Corrie had ever had. Her other teachers hadn't seemed to like children very much. The meanest was Miss Laird. In grade four she had beaten one of the boys over the back with a pointer while the class watched in terrified silence.

Mr. Zelmach was always kind. He called them "ladies and gentlemen," which made them feel important. He was more enthusiastic about music and reading aloud than arithmetic and science. Several times a day he would stop everything and lead the class in a sea shanty or a ballad, whether it was music period or not. They had already begun rehearsing songs for next year's Centennial. "*British Columbia, from the mountains to the sea!*" they shouted. Corrie's favourite was "My Country Is My Cathedral."

Twelve of the girls in grade six were appointed monitors. To Corrie's great surprise, Mr. Zelmach told her she was to be one. That meant she wore a yellow badge and stood in the hall with the rest of the monitors, trying to get all the kids to be quiet as they walked in from recess or lunch. No one ever listened to them, and Juliet stuck her tongue out at Corrie whenever she saw her.

All the other monitors were the popular girls: the Five, plus six girls in 6B. Boys were never monitors; they were considered too irresponsible.

Every morning Corrie had to come into the school early and join the circle of the Five in the hall while they waited for the bell to ring. Corrie never said a word unless someone spoke to her. This was usually Darlene. A long time ago, in grade three, Darlene had been Corrie's best friend. Now she seemed to want to be friends again, as if Corrie's new status made her one of them.

"I really like your kilt, Corrie," she told her one day. Corrie glanced down in surprise. She had two skirts for school that she alternated, this one and a grey pleated one. The kilt had once belonged to Roz; it had moth holes in it, but Darlene didn't seem to have noticed that.

"I really want a kilt, but my mother says she's bought enough clothes for me this fall. Plaid is cool!"

"*I* want a perm, but Mum says I have to wait until grade seven to get one," complained Sharon.

"Grade seven!" exclaimed Gail. "Won't that be great? Is everyone going to Laburnum?"

"I have to go to Ashdown Academy," said Marilyn.

"So do I," said Sharon.

"You poor things!" said Gail. "I'd hate to go to a girls' school. I want to be with boys! Older boys, not the stupid ones in this school."

Corrie wished she could walk away from this disturbing chatter, but she had to wait because she was a monitor.

"Doesn't Meredith wear babyish clothes?" said Donna. "Puffed sleeves and jumpers, as if she was six!"

"And she gets too excited. 'Oh, Mr. Zelmach, that's *so* interesting!'" mimicked Sharon.

Corrie forgot to be shy. "That's not fair! Meredith can't help getting excited, and it's not her fault how her mother dresses her. I think you should be nicer to her! She's my friend, and she's new to this school."

To Corrie's astonishment, they all looked ashamed. "Sorry, Corrie," mumbled Darlene. "We forgot she was your friend, okay?" The others nodded.

The bell rang and Corrie ran to her post. Sebastian would be proud of her—she had been as brave as Sir Gareth!

CORRIE'S FAVOURITE SONG from school was "Men of Harlech"— it sounded like a knights' song. "*Hark!* I hear the *foe* ad*van*cing!" she and Meredith shouted on their way to Meredith's house. They kept stooping to collect shiny chestnuts; by the time they arrived their pockets were heavy with them.

"Sebastian likes to use these for our catapults," said Corrie.

"What are catapults?"

"They're like big slingshots. We made them out of branches and some stretchy rubber Sebastian found. Harry broke a basement window with his, though."

"Oh, *no*! Did your father take the catapult away?"

Corrie laughed. "Fa never knew! In fact, the window's still broken. We patched it with some cardboard."

"I *wish* I could be a knight!" Meredith said when they were settled in her room with cookies and milk.

Meredith said this every day. "I could be Sir Perceval! I've been reading about him—he makes friends with a lion! Why *not*, Corrie? Don't keep saying Sebastian wouldn't like it. He wouldn't ever *know*, so what harm could it do?"

Meredith's eyes shone and Corrie's resistance began to melt. It would be fun to have Meredith as Sir Perceval. They could

make swords to keep at her house and they could design
Meredith a shield. Sebastian would be hurt and furious at her
betrayal. But Sebastian wasn't here, and Meredith was right: he'd
never know.

Corrie grinned. "All right. Shall I dub you? Knights can knight
each other, you know."

"Yes!"

Meredith rushed downstairs and returned slowly with a long
carving knife. She closed the door. "Mum would *kill* me if she knew
I had this, but she won't be back for a while. It'll make a *perfect*
sword."

"I just remembered," said Corrie. "You have to have a trial, like
I did." She thought for a moment. What was Meredith afraid of?

Heights … "Your trial is to climb all the way to the top of your
cedar tree," she said. As Meredith's face whitened, Corrie regretted
her words. She didn't like this kind of power.

But it was too late now. "All right, I *will*! " cried Meredith. She
clattered down the stairs as if she were trying to outrun her fear.

The cedar was huge. Corrie had often climbed to the top herself,
but Meredith always waited below. But today she quickly ascended
until her white face peered down from the top.

"Can I come down?" called Meredith, her voice shaky.

"Yes, come down right now!"

But Meredith looked down and froze. "I *can't*," she said in a thin
voice Corrie had never heard her use before.

"Come on, Meredith, I'll help you. There's a strong branch right
below your right foot."

But now Meredith was crying. "No, I can't! I feel *dizzy*! I'm
going to *fall*!"

Corrie was frantic. What if she did? What if Meredith fell out of
the tree and killed herself? It would be all her fault.

She took a deep breath. *A knight is brave.* She was Sir Gareth, a brave knight of the Round Table.

She forced her voice to be calm. "Master Meredith," she called. "You must not panic. The tree is perfectly safe and you are not going to fall. Remember you are about to be a knight. Do you not want to be one?"

"Ye-es," gulped Meredith.

"Then just come down slowly and carefully and you'll be fine. Start with your right foot.... That's good."

Corrie amazed herself as she guided Meredith down the tree. Her voice was as calm as Sir Lancelot's and it seemed to calm Meredith as well.

Finally Meredith reached the bottom branch and collapsed on the grass.

"Well done, Master Meredith!" cried Corrie. She slapped Meredith on the shoulders. Meredith's cheeks were streaked with tears.

"Oh, Corrie, I was *terrified*! But I *did* it!"

"Yes, you did! Now you can be knighted!"

They ran laughing into the house and back up the stairs. Meredith knelt at Corrie's feet. Corrie tapped the knife on her shoulders as she said solemnly, "I dub thee Sir Perceval, noble knight of King Arthur's Round Table."

"There!" Meredith jumped up, flushed with pleasure. They returned the knife to the dining room and spent the rest of the afternoon making swords out of some scraps of wood they found in Mr. Cooper's workshop.

Sir perceval was a tricky secret to keep. "Is Meredith a knight too?" Orly asked when Corrie and Meredith were galloping down the street on imaginary horses.

Corrie decided it was safer to include Orly and Juliet and Harry in the secret than to try to hide it from them. She took them out to Camelot and made them swear to secrecy on their swords. The twins did this readily, but Harry was reluctant. "If Sebastian doesn't want Meredith to be a knight, I don't think she should be."

"It's just for Meredith and me," Corrie told him. "It's an *extra* game, not the real game. Anyway, she's going to be a knight whether we want her to be or not. And what's wrong with that? Sebastian doesn't need to know."

Finally Harry agreed. Corrie felt only slightly guilty. Mostly she was thrilled to have a fellow knight.

Sir Gareth and Sir Perceval tried to turn their bikes into horses by attaching reins to the handlebars, but it was impossible to ride without falling off. They started a notebook with all their quests written in it. Then they began to pretend school was a school for knights, just as Corrie used to. Whenever Donna or Sharon talked about how dreamy Elvis was, Corrie and Meredith would exchange a smug look. *They* were knights of the Round Table! They would never be that silly.

Corrie reasoned that as long as she kept the two knight games completely separate, everything would be all right. Meredith begged to play with her on Saturday afternoons after Round Table meetings, but Corrie tried to reserve Saturdays for her family.

The school days they played at Corrie's were difficult, however. Then she tried to persuade Meredith to play another game, in case Sebastian came home while she was there.

One rainy afternoon Meredith asked if she could see inside Camelot.

"Camelot!" said Corrie frantically. "No, I'm sorry but—"

"Sebastian wouldn't like it," finished Meredith. "He's out though, isn't he?"

Sebastian had taken Harry on the bus downtown. They wouldn't be back until dinner.

"*Please*, Corrie," begged Meredith. "This could be the only time. I won't touch anything and I won't tell Harry or the twins. I just want to know what's *there*. It would help me to be a better knight, to see all your stuff."

Finally Corrie led her into Camelot, after checking to make sure that Juliet and Orly were safely watching "The Mickey Mouse Club."

"This is *wonderful!*" breathed Meredith. "The table is actually *round!*" She examined everything: the walls hung with coats of arms, the detailed drawings of every part of a knight's armour, and the schedules for jousting and hawking.

"This is my siege," said Corrie proudly, showing Meredith the stool with "Gareth" carved in it.

"Siege?"

"It means seat."

They spent so long in Camelot that Corrie lost track of the time. Suddenly she noticed how dark it was. "Let's go!" she urged. "What if they're back?"

As they burst through the back door, Sebastian and Harry were coming in the front, shaking water from their jackets. "We went to Woodward's, Corrie," said Harry. "Look what I bought with the allowance I saved up!" He pulled a model spaceship from a paper bag. "I didn't have quite enough money, but Sebastian paid the difference."

Sebastian stared at their dripping hair. "Why are you two so wet?"

A knight never lies. Corrie couldn't answer.

"I want to talk to you, Corrie," said Sebastian, looking pointedly at Meredith.

"I'll go home now," said Meredith hastily. "Bye, Corrie. I'll see you tomorrow."

"YOU SHOWED HER *CAMELOT?*" said Sebastian. It had taken only a few seconds for Corrie to confess.

She tried not to cry. "I couldn't help it! She always asks to see it. I finally had to give in."

"*Why* does she ask? How would she know it's anything special?"

"I guess ... because I told her," whispered Corrie.

They were sitting in Sebastian's room. He got up and walked to the window, then turned around. Corrie couldn't bear the hurt look on his face.

"You have betrayed me, Sir Gareth," he said slowly. "You know the Round Table is our secret. This is a very grave matter."

Corrie knew she should answer, "Yes, sire," and wait to hear him pronounce her punishment. But she couldn't help arguing. "Oh, Sebastian, why *shouldn't* Meredith see Camelot? She's my friend! And she really wants to join the Round Table. She'd be great—she knows all about knights and she's brave and chivalrous, and she's—"

"No!" snapped Sebastian. "She can't join us, and that's that! I'm surprised at you, Corrie—surprised and disappointed. I think you should stop being friends with Meredith." He was Sebastian now, not Sir Lancelot—that made his words hurt even more. But Corrie continued to lock her gaze with his.

"I'm sorry," she said steadily. "I won't take Meredith into Camelot again, but I'm not going to stop seeing her. She's my best friend!"

"But you have *us*!" Sebastian's voice broke. "You don't need friends! You have the Round Table! You've never needed anyone else before. First Roz, then you.... What's wrong, Corrie? Isn't this family enough for you? Why are you both being so disloyal?"

Then Corrie melted. "There's nothing wrong, Sebastian," she said gently. "I love the Round Table. I love being Sir Gareth. I won't desert you, I promise. But I *need* a friend. Meredith is the first one I've had for years, and I'm not going to give her up."

"All right." Sebastian tried to smile. "I'm glad you have a friend. As long as you continue to be a loyal knight. And as long as you promise to never let Meredith see Camelot again."

Corrie promised. She left his room with her insides churning. She had meant every word—she didn't want to end her friendship with Meredith. But what would Sebastian think if he knew Meredith was Sir Perceval? Was that being as disloyal as showing her Camelot? How had her life become so complicated?

HALLOWE'EN WAS a welcome distraction. Corrie helped Juliet and Orly create Zorro costumes. Harry was a spaceman. Corrie and Meredith decided to be bookworms. They cut out and painted the sides of a big cardboard box to look like the backs and fronts of books, connected the pieces with string, and hung them over their shoulders. Over their heads they pulled some old stockings of Mrs. Cooper's.

Harry carved the pumpkin to look like Sputnik, and Sebastian bought them firecrackers. Roz declared that she was too old to go trick-or-treating. Instead her club was having a mixed party.

Roz and Joyce had already succeeded in their goal of becoming popular. They had started a club called the Mysterious Eleven. They were eleven girls who met every Saturday night at a different house.

"We're supposed to be cutting up old Christmas cards and pasting them in scrapbooks for the children's hospital," Roz told Corrie. "We don't do that for long—we talk and eat and practise jiving. I don't know what I'll do when it's my turn to have the club here."

"Maybe we could ask Fa to take us all to a movie so you could have the house to yourselves," suggested Corrie.

"But just look at this place—it's such a mess and it smells so musty!" said Roz. The Elephant had practically given up cleaning. She had set up a table with a jigsaw puzzle on it in the corner of the kitchen. When she wasn't reading her magazines she worked at it, the radio turned up so loud that she hardly heard them go in and out. Every surface was thick with dust. When Hamlet wasn't napping, he was kept busy catching mice in the basement or scuttering after silverfish in the bathrooms.

"We could help you clean," Corrie told Roz.

"Thanks, but I'm not going to worry about it yet. It'll be a long time before it's my turn."

Roz continued to tell Corrie about the party. Each of the girls was inviting one boy. "I'm going to ask Ronnie. Do you remember him from my grade six class? The funny boy with the curly red hair? He used to be short and a real pest, always imitating Woody Woodpecker. Now he's grown so tall you wouldn't know him, and he's much nicer. I think he's cute!"

Corrie tried to giggle along with Roz, but it was getting more and more difficult to find something in common with this sophisticated older sister, just as it was with many of the girls in her class. Was there something wrong with her that she wasn't interested in boys or mixed parties or rock and roll?

But neither was Meredith. At least they had each other. It was much more fun to be knights than to moon over some boring boy.

Meredith was enthralled with Hallowe'en in Vancouver. "It's so *different* here! *We* called out 'Hallowe'en apples' in Calgary, not 'Trick or treat.' And we never had *firecrackers*."

Corrie and Meredith covered three blocks of houses, then took home their heavy pillowcases full of candy. They tore off their uncomfortable costumes and went down to the golf course with the others. Orly held Corrie's hand tightly as they stumbled over the grass in the darkness. All around them, neighbourhood kids were setting off firecrackers. Sebastian would only let the twins have little ladyfingers to throw, but Harry was in ecstasy as he heaved cherry bombs into the air. They gasped at the Roman candles whizzing up in balls of colour, then cheered as Sebastian lit the Burning Schoolhouse and it exploded with a satisfying bang.

Corrie's favourites were the sparklers. She waved hers around to make shining streams of light, then wrote "Gareth" in the air. Beside her, Meredith wrote "Perceval." Luckily, Sebastian didn't notice.

6

Mordred

November was crisp and golden. On windy days, leaves and chestnuts showered down from the trees along the Bells' street. Corrie, Meredith, Harry, and the twins raked the leaves over the curb and burned them.

"Hey, Meredith, want to hear our song?" Juliet and Orly began chanting the gruesome song they had been singing since Hallowe'en:

> *The worms crawl in, the worms crawl out*
> *In your belly and out your snout.*
> *Your stomach turns a mushy green*
> *And pus squirts out like whipping cream!*

"We made it up," said Juliet proudly.

"You did not," said Corrie. "We all know that song—it's really old."

"In Calgary we said, 'They eat your eyes, they eat your nose, they eat the jelly between your toes,'" Meredith told her.

Juliet glared at them and retreated to the unraked leaves on the grass, diving into them and emerging like a leaf person.

The chestnuts in the fire of leaves began to pop. "I wish these were the kind of chestnuts you could eat," complained Corrie. All along the block other people were burning their leaves; a curtain of smoke hung over the street.

"My parents would *never* let me make a fire by myself!" said Meredith. "You guys are so lucky your father will let you."

Corrie shrugged. "We've never asked him. It's safe as long as you keep the fire on the street. Harry, let Orly have the rake."

"It's *my* turn!" cried Orly. The two boys tugged until Harry wrenched the rake out of Orly's hands, making him fall backwards. Orly started crying.

"You're such a crybaby," said Harry.

Juliet rushed over from her leaf fort. "He is not!"

"You're always so mean to me!" sobbed Orly.

"You are sometimes, Harry," said Corrie. "It was his turn."

Harry wasn't listening. "There's Sebastian," he said, pointing to a bicycle speeding towards them. "Look at his face!"

Corrie dropped her rake and ran up to the bike. "What happened?"

Sebastian's face was smeared with blood. His nose and one eye were swollen and red. "I don't want to talk about it," he muttered, crashing down his bike. He rushed into the house and slammed the door.

"Se*bas*tian, *bas*tard, Se*bas*tian, *bas*tard!" A group of boys on bikes cycled by slowly with jeering cries. They paused at the house, then rode away, calling again over their shoulders.

Corrie snatched up a hot chestnut and heaved it after them. Then she rubbed her stinging palm and gasped, "How can they treat him like that? Oh, poor, poor Sebastian!"

Meredith patted Corrie's shoulder. "You guys stay with the fire until it's out," Corrie told everyone.

She ran up to the third floor and found Sebastian in the bathroom, dabbing at his nose with a wet washcloth. "I *hate* them!" she cried. She examined Sebastian's swollen nose and eye. "What happened?"

"They called me names, so I told them they were scum.... Then they beat me up."

"Where?"

"Behind the bike stands. They dragged me there. But I ran to my bike and got away," he added proudly. "I think my nose has stopped bleeding."

He sat on the edge of the bathtub as Corrie helped him wipe the rest of the blood off his face.

"You have to *do* something, Sebastian! You have to tell the principal!"

"I can't!" He looked up at her miserably. "You know that, Corrie. They'll just get worse if I do."

"How can they act any worse than they are now! We saw them after you went into the house—they rode by on their bikes and called you names."

"Did they hurt you?" asked Sebastian fiercely.

"No, they kept going." Corrie held the washcloth against her throbbing palm. "There must be someone we can tell. Fa—"

"No! I don't want him to worry about us. I'll figure this out, Corrie." His swollen face hardened. "Terry is my arch-enemy—he is Mordred. I'm going to lie down now, okay?" He left the bathroom, and Corrie heard his door close. She went into the hall and heard muffled noises from inside his room.

A knight never cries. Corrie crouched on the top stair and listened hard, but now his room was silent. She yearned to go into her own room, curl up into a ball, and cry herself, but she had to go out and help Meredith extinguish the fire.

"I think we should tell Fa," she said to Roz that night. Sebastian had stayed in his room all evening; they had told Fa he wasn't feeling well. Corrie took him some food on a tray, but he didn't touch it.

"He would only talk to the principal, and that would make Terry worse."

"That's what Sebastian said," said Corrie. "What can we do, then?"

"Well, Seb could get his hair cut—but he won't. I'm sorry, Corrie. I'd like to help, but this is partly his fault."

"It isn't!"

They argued for a few minutes, until Corrie flounced out, slamming Roz's door. Roz was no use at all these days. She seemed to have forgotten that she was Sir Gawain, Sir Lancelot's closest friend.

All the next day Corrie wrestled with whether or not she should tell Fa. Meredith wanted her to go shopping with her and her mother, but Corrie went straight home after school. She climbed her favourite cherry tree. It was such a safe refuge; people passed by in the lane and didn't even know she was there. When she was younger she had named the tree Sentry, because it seemed to guard the yard. She leaned against Sentry's trunk and her anguish lessened.

I *will* tell Fa, she decided. He's a grown-up—he'll know what to do.

At dinner Sebastian's nose was less red but his eye socket had turned purply-black. Fa's gruff voice rang out. "Look at your face, my boy! Whatever happened?"

Sebastian answered calmly. "I fell off my bike. It looks much worse than it feels."

"You must be more careful," Fa told him. Then he turned to his meal. Corrie gazed fondly at him as he concentrated on each morsel of meatloaf as avidly as he concentrated on his books. It would be nice to talk to him all alone; she hadn't done that for a long time. Perhaps he'd even let her sit on his knee.

Fa was getting balder, she realized. Then she smiled to herself; the less hair Fa had on his head, the more he seemed to have sprouting out of his ears.

When everyone else was safely upstairs doing homework or being bathed, she stood in front of Fa's study, willing herself to knock.

"What are you doing?"

Corrie jumped. Sebastian had come up behind her. "Oh, I was just going to talk to Fa."

"What about?"

Corrie flushed. "Well ..."

Sebastian frowned. "You were going to tell him about me, weren't you?"

A knight never lies. Corrie had to nod.

"Even though I asked you not to?"

"It was for you, Sebastian! It seemed like the right thing to do!"

Sebastian led her into the den. "I appreciate your concern, Corrie, but it's all right now." He told her how Mr. Selwyn, the principal, had taken him into his office and asked Sebastian what had happened to his face. "I told him I'd got into a fight with a guy in my neighbourhood who didn't go to this school. He was very surprised, of course, because I never fight. He gave me a lecture and let me go."

Terry and his gang had seen Sebastian go into the office. They forced him into the boys' washroom and asked if he'd told. "They looked scared," said Sebastian with a smile. "I knew I finally had an edge. They told me that if I had told on them they'd beat me up even more. I said I hadn't, but that I *would* tell—even if they beat me up—unless they left me alone."

"Did they agree?"

"Yes! Well, for a while anyway, Terry said. He hated giving in, but he had no choice. And they avoided me for the rest of the day."

"Touché for you!" cried Corrie.

Sir Lancelot smiled again. "Yes, Gareth—I have won this round. Mordred will strike back, but for now he is at bay."

Corrie went into the kitchen to get an apple. She glanced longingly at Fa's closed door, but now she had no reason to disturb him.

Fa's BIRTHDAY WAS the following Friday. Usually they had a special dinner for him. It was always a surprise because Fa never remembered his birthday.

This year, Sebastian told them he was planning everything himself. "You'll like it," he grinned. "Especially you, Juliet and Orly."

The twins tried to tickle the secret out of him, but he wouldn't tell. Corrie watched with relief. Sebastian's spirits seemed to have healed as well as his face. Now he had only a faint greenish patch under his eye.

They always saved Fa's presents until dinner, since he got up so late. Corrie and Roz had pooled their allowances and bought him a red tartan scarf. Harry had made him a spaceship out of toothpicks, and the twins had coloured a huge picture of a dinosaur.

When Sebastian got home that afternoon, he told them to meet in the hall just before Fa got home at six. "Don't be late!" he warned them.

Corrie wrapped Fa's present carefully. There was still half an hour to wait. She sat in the kitchen and worked on Mrs. Oliphant's puzzle. The Elephant was angry when they touched the puzzle, but it was too hard to resist when it sat there all evening. Once, Corrie and Harry had finished the whole thing. They'd undone all the pieces afterwards, but that didn't mollify her.

The kitchen didn't smell of cooking the way it always did at this time of the day. The Elephant had left at five, as usual. Had she forgotten to make dinner? Corrie peeked in the warming oven—it was empty.

No dinner, and it was Fa's birthday! She reminded herself that Sebastian had said he would take care of everything.

"Hurry up, Corrie, it's almost six!" called Sebastian. She rushed into the hall. "Put on your coats," Sebastian told them.

Fa pushed open the door. "Why, hello, my dears!" he said. "What is everyone doing here?"

"We're going out!" said Sebastian. "To the circus!"

"The circus!" They danced around with excitement, and Fa's round face beamed. He had always loved circuses.

"But, my boy, how on earth did you get tickets? I would have got them for you myself if I'd known the circus was here."

"I won them!" said Sebastian proudly. "There was a raffle at school and I had the winning ticket! The prize was for two people to go. For the rest of the tickets I raked people's leaves and helped Mr. Hanson down the street clear out his garage. That's what I've been doing for the past two weeks when I told you I had a project at school."

"Sebastian, my dear boy—what an incredibly kind and generous thing for you to do! Thank you so much!"

"The only problem," said Sebastian sheepishly, "is that I forgot about dinner. I told the Elephant to put it away, because we don't have time to eat it now. The circus starts at seven, so we have to get the bus right away. Could you all wait until after the circus to eat?"

"Don't worry about that, my boy! I'll buy you all hot dogs or popcorn or anything at all that you want for dinner. And I'll take us there in a taxi so we won't be late."

"You mean I could have *just* popcorn for dinner?" Juliet asked.

"If you like."

"Yay!"

Roz and sebastian had been to the circus before, but the others hadn't. The evening was a thrilling blur of clowns and performing animals and acrobats. From their high seats they oohed and aahed and clapped and shrieked while they wolfed down hot dogs and popcorn and candy floss. Corrie's favourites were the trapeze artists; they looked as if they were really flying. Fa was as excited as they were, pointing out details in each colourful, noisy act. Miraculously, no one was sick.

They got home very late but they stayed up to open Fa's presents. He thanked them all and repeated to Sebastian, "That was such a thoughtful present, my boy—a present for us all. Thank you again."

Sebastian beamed at his family. He was his very best, knightly self tonight, thought Corrie, the way he had often been before he'd started junior high—and before Mum died. If only he could always be this content. If only they all could.

7

The Birthday Party

S ebastian no longer came home beaten up or anxious, so Corrie assumed the bullies were still leaving him alone. He had read a new book about falconry, and the Round Table were all busily making tiny hoods and gauntlets and jesses. They each had an imaginary bird of prey; Corrie called hers Mercury. She and Meredith began to have birds, too. Once in a while each girl would raise her arm in class as if carefully holding a falcon; then they'd exchange secret smiles.

Meredith had been in tears the morning the newspaper said that a dog called Laika had been sent up into space in a Russian satellite. Corrie couldn't comfort her. When Mr. Zelmach asked her what was wrong, Meredith told the class the story. "She's going to *die* up there! They know that, but they still sent her up! It's so *cruel!*"

Mr. Zelmach asked them if they thought it was right to sacrifice an animal for the sake of science. This resulted in such a fervent discussion that it lasted until recess. No teacher had ever let them miss two whole periods just to talk. After that, the class treated Meredith with more respect.

MEREDITH WAS NOW completely besotted with the Bells. "Your family is *much* more interesting than mine," she said constantly. "You're so *different*, like people in a book!" Whenever she came home with Corrie she acted like another sister. She often asked to stay for dinner, but Corrie always discouraged her; she wanted to keep Meredith safely away from Sebastian.

Meredith loved combing Hamlet or persuading the twins to wash their hands. They adored her. If it was Corrie's turn to take them home she sometimes took them to Meredith's house instead.

Mrs. Cooper delighted in the twins also. She made them "Raggedy Ann" snacks: half a peach, a cottage cheese face, shredded carrots for hair, raisins for eyes, and carrot sticks for arms and legs. She laughed when Juliet started calling her Mrs. Coo-coo. Corrie couldn't believe how well-behaved the twins were at Meredith's house. They sat quietly in the Coopers' rumpus room, watching TV and nibbling on their snacks. When it was time to leave they carried up their plates and said thank you.

As Corrie and Meredith were walking to the Bells' house one afternoon, Juliet pranced beside them while Orly ran ahead.

"Brenda asked me to her birthday party!" she exclaimed. "So did Lynn! Can I get presents for them, Corrie?"

"Ask Sebastian for some money," said Corrie.

Juliet had become very popular. Orly had found one friend in his class—Ian, the only little boy who didn't run away from him. But Juliet's toughness and confidence made her the leader of the grade one girls. Every recess Corrie could hear her bossy shrieks to them as she organized their ball-bouncing or skipping.

"Why can't *I* have a birthday party?" Juliet asked.

Corrie was taken aback. "A birthday party! I don't know, Juliet. You'll have to ask Sebastian." Juliet raced Orly to the corner.

"When's their birthday?" asked Meredith.

"November twenty-third. But they've never had a party before. None of us have."

Meredith stopped and stared. "None of you have ever had a *birthday* party? Why *not?*"

"Well, we have family ones," said Corrie. "Just not ones with friends like ... like every one else does," she ended lamely. She had been to lots of birthday parties herself over the years. Not to all of them, of course, but to the ones where mothers insisted on inviting everyone in the class.

"Why *don't* you?" Meredith persisted.

"My ... my mother was always too busy."

Meredith looked nervous. "Mum said I wasn't *ever* supposed to talk to you about your mother. But do you mind if I ask *why* she was too busy?"

Corrie smiled. "I don't mind if we talk about my mother." To her amazement, she really wanted to. Her words rushed out of her like a river overflowing a dam.

"Mum was an artist," she told Meredith. "She had a babysitter for the twins every afternoon and spent all that time painting in her studio. After school we would run up and see what she'd done. Then she'd stop for the day, but that was when she took us shopping or got dinner ready or ..." Corrie's eyes stung.

"Or did the stuff my mum does," said Meredith softly.

Corrie blinked. "Yes. So she was really, really busy. Also, she thought birthday parties were silly." Corrie could hear Mum's musical voice declaring this when Roz had asked for a party. "Roz, my darling, birthday parties are just a circus for a crowd of children to get wild and sick. We'll take you out to dinner instead, all right?"

Corrie had loved the importance of getting dressed up and going out with her family to a fancy restaurant at night. But the older Roz had got, the more she had resented not having normal birthday parties. After Mum died she had organized her own, with Aunt Madge helping. She hadn't had one since Aunt Madge left, though; the house was too messy, and the housekeepers never liked the idea.

"I always have *my* party in September because everyone's away in the summer," said Meredith. "I didn't this year because I didn't know anyone yet. But next year I will—you'll be invited, of course. I know—maybe we can have a *joint* party!"

Corrie smiled at her. "That would be fun."

"Let's have a party for the twins *ourselves*!" said Meredith. "We can have balloons and Pin the Tail on the Donkey and a treasure hunt. Mum could make us a cake. We could even have it at our house if you want," she added with a sideways glance at Corrie.

"But—"

Before Corrie could object, Meredith had called Juliet back and asked her if she wanted to have a birthday party.

Juliet clapped her hands. "Yes! But just for me, not for Orly. He doesn't care about parties, and I only want girls." She and Meredith began discussing plans. They continued up in Corrie's room, making lists of guests and food and games. Corrie finally left them and took a book into the secret cupboard.

Meredith found her there. "What's the matter, Corrie? Don't you want to help us plan the party?"

"I ... I guess so." Corrie knew she didn't want to do it. Was it because Meredith had thought of it and she hadn't? Or because

Mum hadn't approved of birthday parties? Perhaps it was just the change. There was too much of that already this fall. "Let's talk about the party later," she told Meredith. "It's such a sunny day. Do you want to go roller skating?"

Meredith borrowed Roz's skates and they started downstairs. "If your mother was an artist, where are her paintings?" Meredith asked.

Meredith's never-ending curiosity was wearing. "Some are in the living room but most are still in her studio," said Corrie.

"Can I *see* them?"

"We aren't allowed to go into her studio. And I already showed you the living room, the first day you were here," tried Corrie. But Meredith persisted, saying she hadn't looked carefully then.

Corrie led her once again into the dim room. "Can't we open the curtains?" asked Meredith. Without waiting for an answer, she pulled back the heavy velvet curtains that shrouded every window. The room seemed to breathe a sigh of relief as light entered it. Corrie's stomach lurched as the familiar objects came into view.

Mum's vibrant paintings lined the walls. Meredith admired the strong patches of colour arranged in patterns. "But what are they supposed to *be*?" she asked.

Corrie shrugged. "They're called abstracts. Mum said they were more about feelings than things."

She gazed at her favourite: streaks of blue hiding vague grey shapes, the one she used to call *Horses in the Rain*. Corrie remembered Mum laughing as she said, "That's a perfect name for it!"

She was hearing Mum's voice so much today! It was almost as if she were in the room.

Meredith noticed a large photograph on the mantel. She went up to it. "Is that your mother? She's *beautiful*! And look, here's *you*!"

Corrie stood beside her and stared at the photograph. It had been taken before the twins were born. Everyone was sitting on the chesterfield, her parents in the middle. Harry was a fat toddler in Mum's arms. Corrie, aged four, snuggled in Fa's. Sebastian sat beside Fa and Corrie, with one arm resting on his father's knee, smiling sweetly at the camera. Roz, in a smocked dress, her blond hair in pigtails, held Harry's hand. She looked serious for a six-year-old.

Mum's sleek brown hair fell in waves to her shoulders. Her smile was wide and generous. She looked utterly content in the midst of her family.

"You and Sebastian look so much alike! And is that really your *father*?" asked Meredith.

Corrie grinned. "He had way more hair then." She studied Fa's craggy face, so much more focused and happy than it was now. She could almost remember the feeling of being in those sheltering arms.

They drew the curtains closed and went outside. Corrie lifted off the key that hung around her neck and they tightened their skates onto their shoes. They skated down the driveway and Corrie led the way to the Wedds' slanting front path, the smoothest place to skate in the neighbourhood. They each coasted down several times. Then they went around the whole block.

Corrie lifted each heavy foot in turn, letting the even rhythm and the grating sound of the wheels against the pavement soothe her discomfort. Perhaps Meredith would forget about the birthday party.

THAT EVENING AFTER DINNER CORRIE sat at the dining-room table, working on another diorama. This one was a snow scene. She had painted the back of the shoebox blue and pasted white shapes against it to be icebergs. The bottom of the box was lined with pieces of cotton batting. Now she was trying to shape an igloo out of sugar cubes, gluing each one in place after she filed the edges round with a nail file.

Mum was the one who had taught Corrie how to make dioramas. Corrie could still hear her encouraging voice as she showed her how to work from the back to the front. Corrie's first scene was from "Hansel and Gretel." She and Mum had had a wonderful time gluing real candies onto the little cardboard house.

Mum again! Why was she thinking about her so much?

Corrie carefully placed the finished igloo onto the "snow." It looked perfect! She gazed with satisfaction at the contained, safe little world she'd created.

Roz came through the kitchen door with a glass of juice. She slid into the chair beside Corrie.

"That's beautiful! It's your best one yet!"

"Thanks," said Corrie. "I may add some sled dogs or seals."

"Why not some Eskimos as well?"

"Because I don't know how to draw people—you know that! So I just pretend they're inside the igloo."

Roz laughed. Then she said quietly, "Corrie? Do you know what day this is?"

Corrie was trying the igloo in a different place. She shook her head.

"It's the third anniversary of Mum's death."

"Oh!" Corrie whirled around on her chair and stared at her sister. "How do you know?"

"Because I write it down on my school calendar every year. But do you know what?" Now her voice was angry. "No one, not even Fa, has remembered! Or if they have, they haven't said anything."

"I think *I* sort of remembered," said Corrie slowly. "Inside myself, I mean. All day today I've been thinking about Mum and hearing her voice."

"Oh, Corrie, I'm so glad! Everyone else seems to have forgotten all about her! I'm going to too, unless we talk about her, but we never do!"

"We can't," said Corrie. "It would make Fa too sad. Sebastian too."

"Aunt Madge used to talk about her sometimes," said Roz. "I sure wish she hadn't left."

"Me too."

They sat in silence, then Corrie said, "Roz, you can talk to *me* about Mum if you want to. I'd like that."

Roz smiled. "Thanks, Corrie. But I wish we *all* could. Then we'd remember more. It's almost as if Fa and Sebastian are *ashamed* of Mum! Why is it such a secret?"

"I don't know." Corrie looked up hopefully. "So, do you want to talk about her?"

"Not right now. I have too much homework."

Roz left the room and Corrie went back to her diorama. But the icy scene made her feel so cold that she put it away and went to bed.

By the next day it was settled: Meredith said her mother would be delighted to have a party for Juliet at her house.

"Are you sure?" Corrie asked her.

"I'm sure! Mum loves planning parties and she missed doing mine this year. *Please* say yes, Corrie."

Corrie thought of how eager Juliet had looked when Meredith suggested a party. "Okay ..." she said slowly. "It doesn't seem right to have it at your house—she's my sister, after all. But if your mum doesn't mind, I guess we could."

Corrie immediately regretted her decision. For the next two weeks, all Meredith and Juliet could talk about was the party. It was as if Meredith were more Juliet's friend than her own. Juliet crayoned sixteen invitations and delivered them to every girl in her class. Mrs. Cooper found an outgrown frilly yellow dress of Meredith's that fit Juliet perfectly and was in much better condition than Corrie's old dresses. It even had a crinoline. Juliet adored it.

Mrs. Cooper made a *Dick and Jane* cake and decorated the house with pink balloons. She bought pink hats, and Juliet spent hours with Meredith deciding on favours and filling little plastic baskets with candies.

Of course Juliet couldn't help talking about the party at home, even though Corrie begged her not to. Roz said she was glad for her, but Sebastian was upset.

"This won't do," he told Corrie. "Why should Meredith's family have a party for Juliet? We always have a special dinner for her—isn't that enough? Can't you put a stop to it?"

"It's too late," said Corrie. Of course they couldn't stop it, not when Juliet was so excited.

CORRIE WATCHED FROM the kitchen doorway as Mrs. Cooper cut the cake. The seventeen little girls had admired its tiny sugar figures of Dick, Jane, Sally, Spot, and Puff. Now they watched avidly, each one hoping to find a nickel wrapped in waxed paper in her piece of cake. Sunlight poured in the window and lit up the table; it was as if Corrie had frozen the scene in a photograph. Juliet's clean curls glistened around her sharp, intense face. In a few minutes, Corrie knew, her little sister would be roaring around the living room bossing everyone, her face and dress covered with chocolate and her sash undone. But at this moment she looked angelic, as did all of her friends. It was just like a picture in the *Dick and Jane* readers—bright splotches of colour and rosy, happy faces, all too good to be true.

In grade one Corrie had found Dick and Jane so boring that she had sat at her desk and made up more exciting stories for them.

What were Dick and Jane compared to the knights of the Round Table? Corrie threw back her head disdainfully. What was she, Sir Gareth, doing in this bland scene? She missed the usual chaos of family birthday parties. She could hardly wait to get Juliet home to the real party that was waiting for her.

8

Aunt Madge

At the end of November, Fa made an announcement. "I had a letter from my sister. She'd like to come and visit for Christmas. What do you think, my dears, shall we ask her?"

Aunt Madge! Corrie's heart leapt. Aunt Madge phoned on birthdays and holidays, and once in a while she wrote them a letter, but they hadn't seen her for two years.

"Aunt Madge?" asked Orly as if he weren't exactly sure who she was, but Juliet squealed, "Yes, please!" Corrie was amazed that she remembered her. Roz looked thrilled and Harry smiled in his sober way. Sebastian, however, frowned at his plate.

"I don't think that would be a good idea," he mumbled.

"You don't? I must say, I miss Madge. I wish she hadn't had to leave us and look after Daphne, but I suppose she needs Madge more than we do."

Everyone looked guilty except Harry and the twins—they had never known all the reasons why Aunt Madge had left.

"Oh, *please* say she can come, Fa!" begged Juliet. "I like Aunt Madge! She made cookies!"

Roz glared at Sebastian. "Don't listen to Sebastian," she told her father. "We'd love to see Aunt Madge again."

"Why don't you want her to come, my boy?" Fa asked.

Corrie knew he'd never tell. He shrugged, his face down. "It's all right.... She can come. Forget what I said."

Fa looked puzzled, but he was distracted by the rest of them asking when Aunt Madge would arrive. "She wants to come on December twentieth and stay for two weeks," he told them.

"Two weeks! That's too short," said Roz.

Sebastian looked stricken. Corrie knew he thought it was far too long.

"WE HAVE TO CLEAN this filthy house," said Roz the next morning. "Aunt Madge wasn't a very good housekeeper, but even she will be shocked by this." She picked up one of the rolling dust-balls that got bigger and more numerous every day.

"Let's do her room first!" said Corrie.

It took them two weeks. Every day after school they dusted and swept and vacuumed and scrubbed while the Elephant sat over her puzzle and her magazines in the kitchen. Sebastian even cancelled Round Table meetings so they could clean all day on Saturdays as well. They put pails and pails of garbage in the lane and even polished the silver. Meredith helped eagerly.

Surprisingly, Sebastian didn't seem to mind Meredith being there. He was the keenest cleaner of all of them. "I don't want Aunt Madge complaining to Fa that the Elephant isn't doing a good job," he explained to Corrie.

"But she *isn't* doing a good job!" said Corrie. "Oh, Sebastian, couldn't we ask Aunt Madge to come back for good?"

"No! Anyway, she can't. She has to look after Cousin Daphne."

Corrie nodded sadly. She tried to enjoy the fact that they would have Aunt Madge for two whole weeks, instead of remembering that she would then leave.

FOR ALMOST EVERY DAY in December they had clear, frosty weather. Corrie felt more and more Christmassy. In school they were learning from Mr. Zelmach carols she had never heard before: "Lullay Mine Liking" and "In the Bleak Midwinter." On the last day of school they were going to go around to all the other classes and sing to them. She and Meredith pretended that the carol singing was being done for a neighbouring castle.

One evening Sebastian had them all write letters to Santa Claus. Corrie knew that he then took them to Fa.

"Roller skates, two turtles, and a dog," copied Juliet carefully from the words she'd asked Sebastian to print for her.

"Santa won't bring you a dog," Sebastian warned her. "He knows Fa doesn't like them." Fa had told them how he'd been badly bitten by a dog when he was young.

"I know Fa's afraid of dogs, but maybe a *little* one would be okay," said Juliet. "How do you spell 'little'?" She added it in front of "dog."

Corrie pondered her own list. All she could think of was books. Then she remembered something she'd always wanted and added "pogo stick" to her list. Fa—*Santa*, she grinned—might have a hard time finding one, but why not try?

A few days after the house was cleaned, Fa gave Sebastian their usual Christmas money. Sebastian carefully allotted it among them. Roz took Juliet and Orly to Woolworth's and they chose small presents for everyone, making her wait at the front so she wouldn't see hers.

Corrie and Harry rode their bikes up to the stores in the Kerrisdale neighbourhood one Saturday to do their own shopping. They split up, agreeing to meet in an hour.

Corrie found most of her presents in the stationery store. She got a stapler for Fa, crayons for the twins, glue for Harry (he was always running out), an eraser shaped like a butterfly for Roz, and a family of tiny china dogs for Meredith. In a clothing store next door she found a lace handkerchief with an "M" on it for Aunt Madge.

That left Sebastian. He was the hardest because Corrie wanted his present to be perfect. Finally she discovered a small penknife in the hardware store. It cost more than she had left from Fa's money, but she pooled her saved-up allowance with it. Sebastian would love it!

She waited for Harry outside the drugstore as they'd planned. People bustled up and down the sidewalk in front of her, getting ready for Christmas. A Salvation Army band stood on the corner and played "The First Noel." Corrie's cheeks glowed in the frosty air. This week before Christmas was her favourite, with so many treats in store. And Aunt Madge would be here again! Corrie pretended that everything was normal.

Of course, nothing had been normal for three years, not since Mum left them. But at least it could be as normal as possible.

THE FIRST TERM of school ended with a flourish. In November, everyone in 6A had drawn a name. On the last afternoon of school they had pop and cookies while they exchanged their gifts. Corrie received a pink barrette from Jamie. She never wore barrettes, she didn't like pink, and Jamie irritated her; sometimes he called her Freckles. But she was feeling so excited about Christmas that she thanked him politely and put the barrette in her pocket. Juliet or Roz might like it.

Corrie had drawn Deirdre's name and had given her three pencils with her name on them. Deirdre, who had never paid any attention to Corrie, smiled warmly. Sharon was eagerly thanking Meredith for a package of red licorice. Brent pulled one of Carolyn's braids and she didn't even protest. Kathy, Valerie, and Louise started singing, "We three kings of orient are / Trying to smoke a rubber cigar," and everyone joined in. Then Gary and Frank, who were always being hauled into the principal's office for fighting, passed out candy canes arm in arm, saying, "Ho, ho, ho!" Mr. Zelmach had them all bellow, "We wish you a Merry Christmas!" before they scraped back their chairs and dashed out the door into the holidays.

Meredith's family was taking the train to Calgary and staying there until school started. "I'm *so* excited about seeing Sue and Ruthie!" she told Corrie. "I hope we'll still be friends."

Corrie tried to suppress her jealousy. But she was reassured when Meredith gave her an autograph book. It had different-coloured pages. On the first blue one Meredith had written: "On the golden chain of friendship may I always be a link." She seemed to love the china dogs.

CORRIE WAS THRILLED when Fa chose her to go with him in the cab to pick up Aunt Madge. All the way there she struggled to think of something interesting to say. Finally she simply leaned against him. Fa put his arm around her. Corrie pressed her cheek against the prickly tweed of his coat, hardly daring to breathe in case he moved.

The train station was packed with holiday travellers. Corrie and Fa peered into the crowd. Will I recognize her? wondered Corrie. Finally she spotted a tiny figure laden with luggage.

"Aunt Madge!" Corrie dashed to her aunt and was engulfed in her soft fur jacket.

"Corrie! Goodness, how you've grown! And William, my dear, how are you?"

Fa pecked his sister on her cheek and took her heaviest bags. Corrie struggled with two more. She was squished between the two adults on the way back, like a filling in a sandwich.

Fa asked Aunt Madge politely about the weather in Winnipeg and about Daphne, the old cousin she lived with and took care of.

"She's quite a bit better, although her heart still isn't strong," said Aunt Madge. "Her friend Dorothy has moved in with her while I'm gone."

Fa and Aunt Madge had always been formal for a brother and sister. Corrie wondered if they had been like this as children. There were only the two of them; had they been closer then?

Aunt Madge asked about every member of the family. Just as she did on phone calls, Corrie told her an edited version. When she left out Sebastian being bullied and the antagonism between him and Roz, the Elephant's slovenliness and her own worries, their family seemed as smooth and content as the Bobbsey Twins or Dick and Jane. "... And Harry won first prize in the science fair," she finished.

"Did he?" asked Fa with surprise. "Why didn't anyone tell me?"

"We did," said Corrie.

"Dear William, as absent-minded as ever," said Aunt Madge fondly, patting him on the arm. "I'm so excited about seeing everyone again!"

THEY HAD OPENED the curtains in the living room. Now they all sat there, everyone but Sebastian. Orly perched on a stool and gazed at

Aunt Madge suspiciously. Juliet snuggled into her side, wiping her eyes. Juliet rarely cried, but at the sight of Aunt Madge she had burst into loud sobs.

Corrie studied her aunt greedily. She hadn't changed a bit. Aunt Madge wore owlish round glasses and kept wiping back the wispy brown hair that escaped from her bun. She blinked a lot. She wore the same shabby blue tweed suit that she had two years ago, its lapel pinned with a gold horse brooch that had belonged to her mother.

"How clean everything looks!" said Aunt Madge. The living room gleamed with polish; holly was piled on the mantelpiece, and their stockings were carefully draped over the firescreen, ready to be hung up. The neglected room seemed to glow with appreciation.

"You must have a much better housekeeper than I was," said Aunt Madge in a quavering voice.

Juliet sat up, fully recovered. "The Elephant? *She* doesn't do anything!"

Corrie tried to shush her but Juliet continued scornfully. "We cleaned the house all by ourselves! Well, Corrie's friend Meredith helped. Me and Orly dusted every single rung of the banister. It took us hours!"

Luckily Fa didn't seem to hear this. Sebastian had taken him over to examine one of Mum's paintings in the corner of the room. Corrie knew he was avoiding having to talk to Aunt Madge.

"Remember, all of you, you mustn't let on how bad the Elephant is," Sebastian had told them at breakfast. "We don't want Aunt Madge suspecting anything."

"Why not?" said Roz. "Maybe then Mrs. Oliphant would be fired!"

Sebastian had glared at her. "I keep telling you, Sir Gawain. If the Elephant leaves we might get someone who interferes with us too much. Kindly remember that."

Now Corrie thought fast. "We let Mrs. Oliphant go for her holidays early—that's why we all cleaned," she told Aunt Madge. "She *usually* does the housework, of course. And she cooks our dinner every night."

Roz looked as if she wanted to tell Aunt Madge the truth, but Corrie knew she would do as Sebastian wanted.

"Mrs. Oliphant is a terrible cook, though," said Harry. "Can you make macaroni and cheese for us, Aunt Madge, like you used to?"

"And snow pudding!" said Roz.

"And oatmeal cookies!" Corrie remembered.

Aunt Madge laughed. "Hold your horses! Of course I will. I'll make all your favourites." She seemed very pleased that they didn't like Mrs. Oliphant's cooking.

Aunt Madge slipped back into the family as easily as if she'd never left. Orly decided he liked her and followed her around like a puppy. She patiently admired all of Harry's collections and helped Roz shorten her new dress. She even managed to wash Juliet's hair thoroughly.

Aunt Madge took complete charge of the kitchen, and every night they feasted on her roasts and desserts. Corrie and Harry helped her cut out shortbread and ice gingerbread men. She had brought Christmas cake and pudding with her.

One evening they all walked up to the church parking lot, where the Scouts were selling Christmas trees. They took turns dragging their tree home. It reigned over the living room, its branches laden with cranberry chains, bubble lights, and the homemade decorations from school that increased every year. An angel with feathery wings teetered on the top. Now the house smelled of baking and pine needles instead of mould and neglect.

Every night before she went to bed Corrie crept into the room and turned on the tree's lights in the dark. She lay on the floor and gazed up at the soft colours, holding the magic of Christmas to her like a fragile glass decoration that might break.

Presents accumulated under the branches, and the twins spent hours shaking and discussing each one. On Christmas Eve, Aunt Madge cooked tourtière. Then they sat in the living room and Fa read them the last section of *A Christmas Carol* out loud, as he did every year. When Tiny Tim said, "God bless us, every one!" Orly's eyes were closing.

"Off to bed, you two!" Aunt Madge said to the twins. "Harry too."

"Harry's allowed to stay up until eight-thirty now," Sebastian said stiffly.

"But—"

Sebastian frowned, and Aunt Madge stopped talking. Flushing, she helped Juliet and Orly hang their stockings from the hooks under the mantel. Roz brought in the milk and cookies for Santa Claus.

"Do you think Santa will remember my Wild Bill Hickok holsters?" Orly asked sleepily as Aunt Madge led the twins out of the room.

"You'll just have to wait and see!" she told him. She paused at the door. "Goodnight, everyone. I think I'll go to bed myself." She avoided Sebastian's eyes as she blew them all a kiss.

Fa left too, after he had kissed each one of them. "Try to contain the wild hordes until eight," he pleaded to Sebastian.

Corrie turned out the living-room lights. She and Sebastian and Roz and Harry lounged in front of the tree, cracking walnuts and picking out the meat with picks. Hamlet warmed his belly in front of the fire. The flames spat and sizzled and the room was a flickering cave.

"Sebastian," said Harry slowly, "is there really a Santa Claus? I asked Aunt Madge and she said there was. But it's Fa who fills the stockings and brings our presents, right?" He looked at his brother uncertainly.

Sebastian smiled at him. "Aunt Madge thinks you're still a little boy. She doesn't know you're a squire! Squires are old enough to know the truth about Santa Claus. He's not real, Master Harry. He's a story for kids."

Harry looked relieved. "I thought so! Because how could one person go all over the world in one night? And reindeer can't fly, anyway!"

Roz looked worried. "Don't tell the twins he's not real, though. It's nice to believe in Santa Claus when you're their age."

Corrie thought wistfully of when *she* believed, of how she used to stick her head out of her window every Christmas Eve and try to hear bells and hooves on the roof.

"So Santa's a story like the Round Table. Just pretend, I mean," said Harry.

Sebastian frowned. "Well, not exactly. Santa Claus is a myth. The Round Table is more real than that."

"Don't be ridiculous, Sebastian," snapped Roz. "The Round Table is just as much of a myth as Santa Claus is! We *pretend* we're knights—we're not really knights."

Corrie was astonished to see tears in Sebastian's eyes. "I do not like to hear you speaking like this, Sir Gawain," he muttered. He got up and looked at the presents.

Roz looked ready to argue but Corrie grabbed her arm. "It's *Christmas*," she whispered. "Forget about it!"

"Okay. I'm sorry, Sebastian. Let's hang up our stockings and go to bed, okay?"

Corrie's stocking was striped red, green, and white; her name was knitted into the cuff. She wondered who had made it, and decided it must have been Mum.

IN HER SLEEP Corrie felt the most delicious sensation of the year: Fa carefully placing her stuffed stocking over her feet. She turned over, half-awake, making the bell on her stocking jingle.

When she woke up, the full magic of Christmas Day bubbled up in her like sparkling ginger ale. Early sunlight streamed through the window—it was even more perfect not to have rain.

"He came! He came!" Juliet and Orly rushed into her room with their stockings.

"Look what I got, a whole pack of Life Savers!"

"And Silly Putty!"

"And six little cars!"

"And a *tiny* dog, but he's stuffed! I don't mind, though."

"Hold on!" said Corrie through her laughter. "I haven't even seen mine yet!"

They exclaimed at each of her own treats: more Life Savers, a package of coloured pencils and a roll of drawing paper, a pencil sharpener shaped like a cat, a *Superman* comic, a ring with a sparkly blue stone, pick-up-sticks, and red wool gloves. And finishing, of course, with a Japanese orange in the toe.

For the first time, Corrie wondered how Fa knew what they wanted. Did Sebastian and Roz shop for him? Or did he ask store owners what was popular with children?

Right now Corrie didn't need to know; it was more fun to pretend the stockings had been filled by Santa Claus. "Let's go and see what Harry got!" she said, and they rushed down to his room.

At breakfast Aunt Madge gave each of them a kiss. Fa came in, yawning in his shaggy brown dressing gown. It made him look like a bear emerging from hibernation.

"A Happy Christmas to all of you, my dears!" he said.

"Eat fast please, Fa," pleaded Juliet. "We've almost finished!"

When Fa had finally eaten his bacon and eggs they were allowed to go into the living room. Corrie lingered in the doorway, wanting to savour the moment when she first glimpsed the loot under the tree.

A few minutes later she was awash in torn paper, darting arms, and shouts of glee. Orly got his holsters, and the air reeked of caps as he shot off one after the other. Juliet thanked Aunt Madge politely for her Betsey Wetsey doll, but she was far more thrilled with her roller skates. Harry got a chemistry set and Sebastian a large box of poster paints. He thanked Corrie profusely for the penknife. Roz opened a velvet case from Fa containing a short string of pearls. "Oh, Fa, they're beautiful!"

"They were your mother's. You've grown up so much lately, Rosalind, that I thought it was time they were yours."

Roz kissed him quickly. She had tears in her eyes.

"Orly, look! *Turtles!*" Juliet had discovered the bowl on a table.

"Don't maul them," said Sebastian as they each grabbed a tiny, squirming turtle.

At first Corrie didn't think she'd got a pogo stick. She tried to be content with three new books, a View-Master, a paint-by-number kit, and best of all, a tiny stuffed rabbit.

"Perhaps you're too old for stuffed toys, Corrie dear, but it looked so real I couldn't resist it!" said Aunt Madge.

"I love it!" said Corrie. She immediately decided to call the rabbit Pookie, after the books about a rabbit with wings that she had adored when she was little.

Pookie was in a running position, with her ears laid back. Her fur was so realistic, and under her ears was soft pink felt. She was just the right size for Corrie to hide in her hand or put in a pocket.

"Don't forget to look behind the tree, Cordelia," Fa told her. There was the pogo stick! Corrie immediately took it into the hall. To her delight, she managed to jump four times before she fell off.

"Let *me* try!" shouted Juliet.

The only sour note was when Sebastian opened Aunt Madge's present, a crisp white shirt. "I don't know what boys your age like," she said nervously, "but I thought you could always use a new shirt."

"I have plenty of shirts," said Sebastian coldly. "But thank you anyway."

"Seb!" hissed Roz. Corrie glanced at Fa, but he was busy helping Juliet try on her roller skates. Aunt Madge flushed, but she managed to whisper, "You're welcome, Sebastian dear."

Juliet created a welcome diversion when she asked them for suggestions for turtle names. After a lively discussion that included Blondie and Dagwood, Elvis and Everly, the Lone Ranger and Tonto, and Troilus and Cressida, Corrie suggested Tinker.

"That's stupid!" said Juliet.

"No, it's not. Think of Jingle!"

Juliet clapped her hands. "Tinkerbell! It's perfect! But what about the other one?"

"Dumb," said Harry gravely.

"Dumb?"

"Dumb-bell!" They all groaned, but Tinker and Dumb the turtles remained.

"It's almost time for church," said Sebastian. "Who will help me gather up the paper?" The younger ones competed to stuff all the paper into the basket by the fireplace. Reluctantly they left the array of presents under the tree and went to get dressed.

There was no Sunday school today. Corrie liked staying peacefully in church the whole service, safe in the middle of her family. She kept touching Pookie in her pocket. The organ played her favourite carol, "Silent Night," as she watched Sebastian and Roz return from Communion. Roz looked around for friends from school, but Sebastian was solemn. Coloured patches from the stained-glass windows shone on his face, and Corrie shivered. Knights took religion very seriously; Sir Lancelot had told them the story of the Holy Grail. Sebastian looked so pure and holy, as if he were really Sir Lancelot attending Mass before a battle.

In two years *she* would be confirmed and could take Communion as well. Corrie wondered if she would like it; she didn't care at all for the taste of wine.

THE REST OF CHRISTMAS DAY was a happy blur ... Playing with their presents under the tree. Helping Aunt Madge set the table and stir the gravy. Pulling crackers and giggling at Fa with a pink paper hat perched on his bald head. Stuffing themselves with turkey, mashed potatoes, turnips, and Brussels sprouts. Singing "We All Want Figgy Pudding" as Aunt Madge proudly brought in the flaming dish. Finding a tiny bit more space for the heavy pudding with its sweet hard sauce. Collapsing and groaning in the living room in front of the fire. Playing charades. Helping Aunt Madge do the dishes. And, finally, everyone stumbling up the stairs to bed, Fa and Sebastian each carrying a sleeping twin.

It had been an almost perfect Christmas Day. Sebastian hadn't clashed again with Aunt Madge, and he and Roz had been friendly. Best of all, Fa had been present each moment.

Corrie sank into sleep, clutching Pookie. If only the magic could last forever.

9

False, Miscreant Knight

*U*sually holidays were Corrie's favourite times. Sheltered from the outside world, she could nuzzle into her family the way she burrowed into her eiderdown on chilly nights. And Sebastian was always happiest on holidays, able to devote himself more to being Sir Lancelot.

Every New Year's Day the knights of the Round Table enacted the story of when young Arthur pulled the sword from the stone. It took place at a grand ceremony, so they had to be ready for it. This year they were making banners for each knight. Sir Lancelot said the squire and the pages could also carry banners. They spent hours in Camelot, cutting the banners out of white cardboard and decorating them with Sebastian's new paints.

Corrie loved the medieval names for the colours: the two metals, "or" and "argent," and the tinctures, "azure," "vert," "sable," "gules," and "purpure." Sir Lancelot drew them a page of symbols and each person was allowed to choose his own. Sir Gareth decided on a star in argent, with a sable dog and wavy lines in azure. Master Jules did his entire banner in a bright rainbow and got angry when Master

Orlando copied it. They fastened the banners to long sticks of bamboo.

Roz had not attended one Round Table meeting that week; instead, she spent every day at Joyce's house.

"I have made a beautiful banner for you, Sir Gawain," Sir Lancelot told her one day in the den. "You will be here for the ceremony, will you not?" He looked worried rather than angry.

Roz tossed her head. "I suppose so, if I must." She flounced out the front door before Sebastian could reply. Corrie, listening on the stairs, shivered at the bitterness in her voice.

"What are you all doing out there in the shed every day? I hardly see any of you," said Aunt Madge when Corrie came in to get more water for painting.

Corrie squirmed. Last week they had spent every moment with Aunt Madge getting ready for Christmas; there had been no time for the Round Table. "We're just playing. You know ..."

Surely Aunt Madge remembered. They had never talked to her about the Round Table, but when she lived here she had often seen them prancing around on their horses or having sword fights in the yard.

"I know," sighed Aunt Madge. "You're still playing knights. Corrie, dear, I'd like to talk to you about that while I'm here."

"I can't right now. They're waiting for me." She left before Aunt Madge could say any more.

BUT THAT EVENING, while the others were watching *The Three Musketeers*, Aunt Madge asked Corrie to help her wind some wool in her room. Sebastian glanced up suspiciously as Corrie left. She smiled to reassure him.

It was so pleasant to be once again sitting on Aunt Madge's bed while Aunt Madge sat in her low chair with her knitting. Corrie had had many comfortable conversations in here. She had listened to stories of the small town in England where Aunt Madge and Fa grew up, and of the years Aunt Madge had spent as a matron in a boys' school in Winnipeg. They had discussed how to solve Orly's fear of the dark and Juliet's nail-biting.

Aunt Madge had always confided in Corrie more than the others. "You remind me so much of my dear mother," she always said.

Corrie wished she remembered her grandmother. She was the only person her age she knew who didn't have grandparents. Fa seemed more like a grandfather than a father; he was almost old enough. Thinking of him this way made his detachment seem more normal.

"Corrie dear, there are a few things I'd like to discuss with you," said Aunt Madge timidly.

"What things?" asked Corrie, just as nervous.

"First of all, I want to tell you why I left two years ago."

Corrie gulped. "I thought it was because of Cousin Daphne being sick."

"It was. But it was also because of Sebastian."

"I don't think we should talk about that," said Corrie quickly.

"I think we have to," said Aunt Madge, unusually firmly. "I've thought about this ever since I left. Just hear me out for a few minutes, dear."

Corrie wished she could run out of the room.

"Sebastian has never liked me," said Aunt Madge. "He was angry with me as soon as I arrived to help. It's because he thought I was trying to take the place of poor Molly, of course. He and Molly were so close—do you remember?"

Corrie dimly did. Mum and Sebastian had spent hours painting together. Sebastian had a real talent, she'd said. But now the only time Sebastian painted or drew was for knight projects.

"It's natural for an eleven-year-old boy who's just lost his mother to be angry about anyone else trying to take care of him. I understood that. And except for a few outbursts, he kept his anger to himself. I thought he would get over it, and I thought I would only be with you for a year. But when your father asked me to stay, Sebastian's reaction became so extreme and so—so hurtful. In the end he made my life miserable, as you may remember."

Corrie squirmed. As soon as Fa had told them that Aunt Madge was going to live with them permanently, Sebastian had begun his campaign.

At every meal, except for dinner with Fa, Sebastian had asked Aunt Madge terrible questions. "Aunt Madge, dear," he would say sweetly, "why didn't you ever get married? Couldn't you find a man who liked whiskers? ... Phew, something smells! Aunt Madge, have you ever thought of using Odo-Ro-No?"

Aunt Madge would gasp and blush, and sometimes her eyes would well up. If she asked Sebastian to do something he would answer coldly, "Why would I choose to do that?" in a sarcastic tone none of them had ever heard before.

Corrie and Roz had tried to talk to Sebastian. But he had ignored them. "Aunt Madge is Morgan La Fay. She is evil and must be vanquished."

"But *why?*" Roz had asked. "She's really nice and you're being so rude! You've got to stop!"

But Sebastian's cruelty had remained ruthless. Corrie remembered how desperate he seemed. It had lasted only a week, but it was one of the longest weeks of Corrie's life.

Roz had come up to Corrie's room every night and they had lamented together over Sebastian's behaviour. Corrie thought they should tell Fa, but as usual he was so immersed in his work that they hated to disturb him.

"Anyway," Roz had said, "I couldn't bear for him to know how awful Sebastian is being. What's wrong with him, Corrie? It's as if he's a different person!"

Then Cousin Daphne had phoned and Aunt Madge had announced that she had to leave to take care of her. Corrie had felt so relieved that the torture would be over that she had forgotten how much she would miss her aunt.

It had probably been a relief to Aunt Madge as well, Corrie thought now. Would she have stayed if Cousin Daphne hadn't been sick? Maybe she would have spoken to Fa and they would have confronted Sebastian.

"I'm sorry, Aunt Madge," Corrie whispered. Her eyes prickled. "I'm really sorry Sebastian was so mean to you."

Aunt Madge put down her knitting, pulled Corrie to her chair, and held her against her tweedy front. "It's all right, dear girl. He didn't intend to be, I'm sure. He was so unhappy about his mother's death, he couldn't help it."

Corrie sniffed in the soothing smell of 4711. She yearned to weep and be comforted even more. *A knight never cries.* Corrie forced back her tears and sat up.

Aunt Madge picked up her knitting again. "What worries me, Corrie dear, is that Sebastian still resents me. I was really hoping that he would accept me now, but he can't seem to do that. You see, Daphne is getting stronger every month. If the day came when she didn't need me any more, perhaps ... Well, I was really hoping I could come back."

"Come back! Oh, Aunt Madge, do you really think you could?"

"There's nothing I'd like better. I miss you all so terribly—there's scarcely a moment in the day when I don't think of you. The problem is ..."

"Sebastian," said Corrie glumly.

"Yes, Sebastian. Would he be the same if I came back? Would he still resent my being here? I don't know if I could bear him behaving the way he did before, and I wouldn't want to make him unhappy."

Corrie's head whirled. Probably Sebastian would be even worse if Aunt Madge came back. He was used to being in charge now, to controlling their lives, from bedtimes to allowances. She couldn't imagine him changing. She thought of the bliss of having Aunt Madge living here again, and for the first time in her life, she felt angry at her brother.

"I don't know why Sebastian is the way he is," she mumbled.

"Well, he's at a difficult age. I'll just keep trying to be friends. He can't hold out forever, can he? Anyway, Daphne may not get better and I may not be able to come back. I probably shouldn't have told you that, Corrie. I'm sorry I got your hopes up."

Corrie tried to smile. "That's all right."

Aunt Madge put down her knitting and sat up straighter. "Now, Corrie, there's another matter I want to discuss. It's about your game of knights."

Immediately Corrie was on her guard. The Round Table had nothing to do with the grown-ups, not even nice ones like Aunt Madge.

"Sebastian has pretended he was Sir Lancelot ever since he was a little boy," said Aunt Madge. "Your mother used to call him her knight in shining armour."

"She did?" Corrie had never known that Sebastian was a knight before Mum died.

"After Molly's death Sebastian gradually enlisted Roz and you and Harry into his game. It seemed to comfort him, and as long as he was still a child his game seemed normal, just pretending, as all children do. But, Corrie, I can't help noticing how much being knights seems to have taken over your lives. Sebastian is fourteen! It's not healthy for a teenaged boy to immerse himself in fantasy like this. Roz knows that. She's growing up, she's making new friends and having the normal interests of a teenager. But Sebastian is retreating from reality, and all of you except Roz are doing the same. None of you seem to have any friends or interests outside of the family."

"But I *have* a friend now!" said Corrie. "Her name is Meredith. You haven't met her because she's away for the holidays. Orly and Harry have friends at school, and Juliet is the most popular girl in her class!"

Aunt Madge smiled at her. "I'm glad to hear it. But I still don't think this game is good for you. You all seem obsessed by it. I think it's time Sebastian put an end to the knights."

"No!" Corrie cried.

"Hush a moment, dear. Just hear me out. I tried to talk this over with William yesterday. He was no help at all. He said Sebastian seemed happy enough and he admired Sebastian's grasp of the Middle Ages! I think *you* have to say something to Sebastian, Corrie. I know how close you are to your brother."

Aunt Madge smiled. "I used to be that close to William, too. *We* played a game for years: we pretended we were Greek gods. He was Apollo and I was Pan. But then William went away to school, and when he came home he was so immersed in literature and his new brainy friends that he hardly spoke to his dull little sister."

She sighed, then turned to Corrie with a determined look. "Corrie, dear, I think you should suggest to Sebastian that he end this foolish game. Couldn't you do that? You could still play knights with your new friend and with the younger ones. But there's something wrong with a boy Sebastian's age being so childish."

A foolish game? The Round Table? Corrie stood up and said stiffly, "I'm sorry, Aunt Madge, but I can't ask Sebastian to do that. And there's nothing wrong with him!"

"Are you sure?" said Aunt Madge softly. "Is he still being bullied? I remember just before I left, when Sebastian started junior high. Some rough boys used to follow him home from school and taunt him."

"They don't do it any more," said Corrie. That was the truth, at least. She took a deep breath. "Sebastian has good friends now ... he's popular! The game is only for home. I don't see what's wrong with it."

"He has friends? Why isn't anyone phoning him, then? Why isn't he seeing them this week the way Roz is seeing hers?"

"They're all ... away. His two best friends are skiing and the other one has gone to ... to Hawaii," said Corrie frantically.

A knight never lies. But surely a knight had to lie to save the Round Table.

To her amazement Aunt Madge seemed to believe her. "I'm so relieved to hear Sebastian has friends, Corrie. Well, perhaps I'm worried for nothing. But I do wish he'd cut his hair in a more normal way."

"He isn't normal! He's special! He can wear his hair any way he likes!"

"I agree that he's special, Corrie. He always has been. He's an extremely intelligent and gifted young man. And I know how much you admire him. Would you let me know if he gets isolated? Then I'll try to approach your father again."

Corrie nodded because she had no choice. "Can I go and watch TV now?"

"Of course you can! I'm glad we had this talk, dear. And if Sebastian is happy at school and has friends, I suppose it's all right. Probably he just plays the game at home to please the rest of you. He won't do it for long, I'm sure. Wait until he discovers girls!"

Aunt Madge seemed to be trying to reassure herself. Corrie left her. She went to her room instead of downstairs and lay trembling on her bed. If the Round Table ended, all their safety, the refuge they had sheltered in since Mum's death, would disappear.

She opened up the *Happy Hollisters* book she had received for Christmas and immersed herself in the senseless but soothing adventures of an impossibly contented family.

"LET US NOW RELIVE the glorious moment of honour for our beloved king," intoned Sebastian. Corrie shivered, and not just from the chill of the shed; she adored this ceremony.

They were all dressed in their best armour or tunic. Picking up their banners, they mounted the horses that had newly braided reins for the occasion and waited for Sir Lancelot's signal. Corrie kept glancing at Roz. It was a relief to see her in Sir Gawain's usual garb—a chain-mail shirt fashioned out of netting that Roz had painted silver the year before. Roz seemed to be as absorbed as the rest of them, but her face was so blank it was hard to tell.

"We will begin!" said Sir Lancelot. They paraded out of the shed and around the yard. Corrie imagined how Lightning tossed his noble head, how the crowds cheered wildly; she almost waved to them. When she glanced at the kitchen window she noticed that Aunt Madge was watching. Corrie tried not to look back.

The procession stopped at a boulder half-submerged in the farthest part of the yard. On top was an inverted tin washing tub, and from a slit in it protruded a huge wooden sword.

They held their horses still and stood, transfixed, while Sebastian told them the familiar story of how the sword had been stuck into a steel anvil that lay on a slab of stone in a London churchyard. Written on the stone in gold letters were the words: WHOSO PULLETH OUT THIS SWORD OF THIS STONE AND ANVIL IS RIGHTWISE KING BORN OF ALL ENGLAND.

Corrie could see the story as clearly as if it were happening right in front of them. How Sir Ector, his son, Sir Kay, and his foster son, Arthur, came to London to joust on New Year's Day. How Sir Kay forgot his sword and sent Arthur back for it. On his way Arthur spotted the sword in the churchyard. "With one heave he lightly pulled the sword out of the stone," said Sebastian. He drew the sword out of the stone himself and they all cheered. "Thus was Arthur recognized as the rightful king of England!" Sebastian looked so majestic himself, he could just as easily be young King Arthur as Sir Lancelot, Corrie decided.

"And now, one more time around, my brave company, and then we shall feast!" They pranced back to Camelot. This feast was even grander than October's: cold turkey, ginger ale for mead, Christmas cake, and nuts.

"I wish we could eat with our hands all the time," said Orly, dangling a long piece of turkey and eating it from the bottom up.

"Now that we have feasted, perhaps Sir Gawain could entertain us," said Sir Lancelot. Sir Gawain was known for his prowess on the harp. Last year he had made one out of wires stretched across a wooden box.

Sir Lancelot handed the harp to Sir Gawain. But instead of taking it, Roz stood up and went to the door.

"I have something to tell all of you," she said. Her face was white and her voice shook. "Especially you, Sebastian. I'm not going to be a knight any more. I'm too old for it. It's just a game—a game for kids. You're too old for it too, Sebastian. Why don't we just let the younger kids play it?"

Sebastian had turned as white as she was. "Do I hear you rightly, Sir Gawain?" he whispered.

"I'm not Sir Gawain any more! You heard me—I'm done! I'm never going to play your silly game again!" Roz ran out of the shed, slamming the door behind her.

The rest of them sat in shocked silence.

"Never mind," muttered Sebastian at last. "Pay no heed, fellow members of the Round Table, to what Sir Gawain has said. He is a false, miscreant knight." His voice was so cold that Corrie winced.

"What does that mean?" asked Juliet in a scared voice.

"It means that Sir Gawain is evil and disloyal. He is no longer one of us—he is banished."

"Do you mean Roz is going away?" asked Orly. He stood up and looked at the door.

"It's all right, Orly," Corrie told him. "It just means Roz isn't going to be a knight any more. She's still part of the family. She's still our sister."

"But why isn't she going to be a knight?" asked Harry.

"Because she has chosen not to be," said Sebastian bitterly. "Lately Sir Gawain has seldom been here anyway. We can easily do without him. Master Harry, help me carry out his siege."

Harry helped Sebastian pick up the stump with "Sir Gawain" carved in it. They took it outside and threw it into the bushes at the back of Camelot.

The celebration was ruined. Orly started crying and Sebastian let him go back to the house. Harry and Juliet continued to look scared and Sebastian pressed his lips closed. Silently they gathered up the fragments of food and took them into the kitchen.

Sebastian went up to his room with a heavy tread. They could hear his door slam.

"What's the matter?" asked Aunt Madge, stirring cake batter. "Have you had an argument? First Roz is upset, then Orly, and now Sebastian!"

"It's nothing," Corrie muttered. She took Juliet by the hand, went to find Orly, and played Fish with them until dinner.

SEBASTIAN SPENT MOST of the last days of the holidays sequestered in his room. He was drawing a book of birds of prey, he told Corrie. At meals his face was tight and his voice strained. Corrie didn't dare bring up Roz's disloyalty.

Roz, on the other hand, seemed at peace with herself. Corrie realized how torn she must have felt in the past months, how drawn to both the Round Table and her life at school. Now she could devote herself entirely to being a teenager.

She began to keep the radio continually tuned to a rock-and-roll station. Songs like "Jailhouse Rock" and "Wake Up Little Susie" boomed through the house. Roz raved about Elvis to Corrie.

"He's so dreamy!" she said.

"He's awful!" shuddered Corrie. The singer's slimy hair and the knowing grin on his face scared her.

"You're just like I was, Roz," laughed Aunt Madge. "For me it was Frank Sinatra. How I worshipped him! I still do, I suppose."

The night before she left, Aunt Madge took them all—except Sebastian, who refused to go—to *Around the World in Eighty Days*. Luckily the others chattered to her so much that Corrie didn't have to. She had avoided her aunt ever since their talk. She hated the hurt looks Aunt Madge gave her, but she just couldn't risk talking about Sebastian or the Round Table again.

Now she was in the hall, saying goodbye. This time Roz was the one going in the cab.

"Oh, my dears, how I will miss you all!" Aunt Madge's eyes glistened as she kissed each of them. Sebastian even smiled, he was so obviously delighted she was leaving.

Corrie's own eyes were moist as she felt the soft body embrace her. "Don't go!" she wanted to cry.

The house felt desolate when Fa and Roz got back. Tomorrow the Elephant would return and school would begin again. What had happened to the magic of Christmas?

10

The Kingdom of Cordith

Fa didn't notice, of course, that Sebastian and Roz were now like strangers. They talked only when they had to, in coldly polite words. Corrie found herself longing for their arguments. At least then they were themselves.

Corrie didn't realize how much she'd missed Meredith until their reunion. "Oh, Corrie, I got a *budgie!*" she cried when Corrie met her at the corner as usual. "His name's Paisley and he's *gorgeous.* Can you come to my house today and meet him?"

After school Corrie and the twins sat in the Coopers' kitchen and admired Paisley. He *was* gorgeous, with bright blue markings and speckled wings.

"He won't *talk*," complained Meredith.

"You have to sit by his cage and repeat something over and over," Corrie told her. "That's what Roz did."

They left the twins chattering to Mrs. Cooper and went up to Meredith's room. After Meredith had finished telling her all about Calgary, Corrie related the story about Roz leaving the Round Table.

At once Meredith begged again to join. *"I* could be Sir Gawain! He's an important knight—you'll need him."

"You know Sebastian won't let you."

"Then I'll be Sir Gawain instead of Sir Perceval when we play knights here," said Meredith.

"That's something I've been thinking about, Meredith," said Corrie slowly. "I don't think you and I should be knights any more. Sebastian would be really mad if he knew."

"But he *won't* know!"

"I still don't want to," Corrie said stubbornly. "It doesn't seem right."

"But *why?*"

"I can't explain. I just don't want to, okay?" Being knights outside the family now seemed as false and miscreant as Roz's disloyalty.

Meredith kept arguing, and both of their voices became angry. Corrie got so tired of repeating herself that she finally rushed out of the room, grabbed the surprised twins, and walked home. She stumbled through the rest of the day, trying not to think about Meredith until she was in bed.

She had lost her best friend! *A knight is loyal.* Ever since Roz had abandoned them, Corrie had realized how disloyal she had been, playing knights behind Sebastian's back. Sir Lancelot needed to count on Sir Gareth more than ever, now that he was the only other knight left.

Why couldn't Meredith understand that? The thought of never playing with her again, of never again going to that welcoming house, was unbearable.

A knight never cries. Corrie swallowed her tears, pushing down another disloyal thought: If there wasn't a Round Table, she wouldn't have this conflict.

"I'M SO *SORRY,* CORRIE," said Meredith immediately the next morning. "I don't understand why Sebastian has this power over you, but he's your *brother.* If *I* had a brother maybe I'd be the same. We don't have to play knights any more."

Corrie was so relieved, all she could do was stand there and grin.

That day after school they started a new game—dressing up their small stuffed animals. Corrie only had Pookie, but Meredith lent her the squirrel and two of the teddy bears.

Meredith had already named the raccoons Raccy and Coony. They called the squirrel Perri, after the movie. The four bears were Edward, Oscar, Simon, and George.

Mrs. Cooper had a large basket full of sewing material. For hours Corrie and Meredith fashioned tiny capes trimmed with sequins, and hats that fastened with embroidery floss and had slits for the animals' ears. Pookie's hat had a tiny bell on top.

On the days when it was dry enough to play outside, they made twig houses and leaf beds for the animals in the Coopers' rock garden. They circled an area with stones and called it the Kingdom of Cordith, from their two names. The four bears were the kings, the raccoons were princes, and Pookie was a princess.

All of the animals could fly. Corrie and Meredith chose one each day to take to school. They soared them through the air on the way, but as soon as they came within sight of the building they hid the animals in their jacket pockets.

At first the animals stayed there during class. Then, because neither girl had pockets in her skirt, they sewed pouches and hung the animals around their necks.

This was Meredith's idea; Corrie was worried that someone would notice, but Meredith told her what to do. If someone asked, "What's that around your neck?" then Corrie was to shrug and say nonchalantly, "Oh, nothing." She got used to it, and began to enjoy the power their mystery created.

One day at recess the Five circled them. Donna smiled. "We can't stand the suspense any longer! Could you *please* show us what you have around your necks?"

Meredith giggled. "What do you think, Corrie? Shall we *tell*?"

"I ... guess so," faltered Corrie. What if they thought they were impossibly childish for playing with stuffed animals?

But the five girls shrieked with delight when they saw Pookie and Raccy. They admired their capes and stroked their furry heads.

The next day Darlene brought a tiny mouse dressed in a red cape. Donna had a giraffe, and Gail a fox terrier. Because they displayed their animals proudly on their desks, Corrie and Meredith let theirs out of their pouches. It was much easier to endure arithmetic with Pookie perched on the inkwell.

Within two weeks every single girl in the class had brought a small stuffed animal in costume to school. Mr. Zelmach decreed that the animals were allowed to sit on the desks, but no one was permitted to pick them up or play with them during class.

Soon the other grade six class, and some of the grade fives, had animals as well. All of recess was taken up with introducing and comparing the animals. "We've started a *fad*!" gloated Meredith.

The best part was that Corrie and Meredith still had their secret game. All the girls delighted in naming and dressing their animals, but no one knew about the Kingdom of Cordith and the increasingly elaborate stories that Corrie and Meredith made up about it.

For Corrie, the new game became a welcome refuge. She paid Harry a month's allowance to take home the twins two more days a week. It was hard to give up her comic and candy money, but worth it. Now she played at Meredith's almost every afternoon. Even on Thursdays, when Meredith rode her bike to her piano lesson, Corrie stayed at her house, helping Mrs. Cooper get dinner ready.

Meredith's mother was so easy to be with. She talked to Corrie as if she were grown up, telling her how much she missed her parents in Calgary. "We're trying to persuade them to move here, but they won't budge!" she lamented.

Mrs. Cooper gave Corrie a whole bagful of shoeboxes to use for dioramas. "Is everything all right, Corrie?" she sometimes asked. Corrie assured her it was. She bent her head over the counter to hide her shame that, once again, she had to lie.

EXCEPT FOR the Round Table meetings, which still happened every Saturday, orderly life at home had fallen apart. This was because Sebastian had changed. One week in late January he suddenly seemed so much happier that at first Corrie thought he and Roz had made up. But the two of them still ignored each other.

Sebastian sat at the table with a faraway look in his eyes. He whistled constantly. And at every meeting of the Round Table he read them stories about Guinevere.

"'He loved the queen again above all other ladies and damsels all the days of his life, and for her he did many great deeds of arms, and saved her from the fire through his noble chivalry,'" he quoted in a tender voice.

"That's too mushy," complained Orly.

"No it's not!" said Juliet. "Guinevere's brave, isn't she?"

Sir Lancelot smiled at her. "She is the bravest and most beautiful woman in the world, Master Jules."

Sebastian became more and more absent-minded. He didn't react when Harry missed his turn drying dishes or when Juliet turned her porridge bowl upside down on the table. He forgot to give them their allowances. He even forgot his own birthday. When they gave him their presents at the breakfast table he smiled with surprise.

Roz was out almost every evening now, doing her homework with Joyce. Sebastian went straight to his room after dinner and neglected to enforce bedtimes. The others stayed up later and later, watching TV shows Sebastian had never let them watch. Roz got home about nine and crossly ordered them all to bed. In the mornings they yawned heavily and protested about having to get up.

Corrie turned out her light later and later. She found it hard to concentrate in school, and occasionally she fell asleep on Meredith's bed. Orly had blue circles under his eyes and he burst into tears about the tiniest things. Juliet started a fist fight with another girl and had to go to the principal's office.

After Harry told her that he had got into trouble for falling asleep on his desk, Corrie decided she would have to be the one to set bedtimes. That night she insisted that the twins go to bed at eight as usual, and Harry at eight-thirty. Despite regretting the missed reading time, she made herself turn her own light out at nine.

"I'M *ITCHY*," complained Juliet one morning, scratching some red spots on her face.

"Oh, no!" said Roz. "Chicken pox!"

"How do you know?" Corrie asked her.

"Because Harry had it two years ago—don't you remember?"

Corrie nodded. "What should we do?" Usually Sebastian would have a suggestion, but he had left for school early.

"Put her to bed and call the doctor, I guess."

"But who will take care of me?" demanded Juliet, proud to be so important. The others pondered this. Before the twins went to school, the housekeeper—or, before that, Aunt Madge—took care of anyone who was sick.

"The Elephant will be here," said Harry.

"You know she won't take care of Juliet." Roz looked defeated. "I'll have to stay home from school. And I have a math test today! And I'll miss baton practice!"

"*I'll* stay home," said Corrie.

"Me too!" offered Harry.

"Don't be ridiculous. You're far too young!" Roz snapped. Then her eyes filled with tears. "I'm sorry, you guys, I didn't mean to yell at you. But it's so hard! What if Juliet is sick for a week? What if Orly gets it? He probably will; he's the only one of us who hasn't had it. What are we going to do?" Then she cried in earnest, putting her head on the table. "It's not fair! I'm so tired of trying to look after everyone, especially since Seb is doing *nothing* these days."

Harry patted Roz's back awkwardly while the twins watched with frightened eyes.

"*Fa* should look after her," said Corrie. "I'm going to wake him up and tell him."

Roz raised her wet face. "Don't, Corrie! He has to go to work!"

"He's our *father*," said Corrie, in a firm voice that seemed to belong to a stranger. "He's *supposed* to look after us."

She ran to Fa's study and knocked on the door. After a minute he opened it, yawning and engulfed in his dressing gown. "I'm sorry to bother you, Fa, but we think Juliet has the chicken pox and we have to go to school."

Fa shook his head awake. "Chicken pox!" In a minute he was in the kitchen, examining Juliet. "Now don't you worry about a thing," he told them, as focused as he was on Sundays. "I'll phone the doctor and put her to bed. You'd better stay home as well, young Orlando, since you're bound to get it. Hop into your beds, you two. I'll come up in a moment and read you a story until the doctor comes."

"But, Fa," said Roz, "what about your classes?"

"I'll phone and cancel them. Off to school with all of you, now, before you're late." He shooed them out the door.

When Corrie got home, Orly had broken out into spots as well. Both twins were feverish and whiney, their room a mess of drinks, toys, and rumpled sheets. Fa looked rumpled and exhausted himself, but he refused to let any of them help. "Doctor Blair said it was normal childhood chicken pox. They'll be fine in about a week."

"A week! Can you stay home all that time?" Corrie asked him.

Fa smiled. "It's all arranged. I have a teaching assistant to take my classes—it will be good for him. And when the twins are napping or watching television I can work a little on my book."

"But ... do you *want* to look after them all day? Maybe you could pay the Elephant extra to take care of them."

"Mrs. Elephant has made it very clear that she doesn't want any extra work. She's a rather touchy woman, isn't she? But never mind, I'm quite happy to stay home. We've been having a good time, haven't we? We've read some of the *Just So Stories* and we're about to start *The Water Babies*. We've played Fish and Slapjack, we've built a Tinkertoy castle, and we've drawn pictures of knights and dragons."

"We have a *pox*, Corrie," said Juliet. "We may die!"

"Nobody is going to die, Juliet dear," said Fa. He rubbed some pink lotion onto her cheeks. "Now, remember not to scratch." He picked up Juliet, and surprisingly for her, she leaned her hot head against his shoulder. Lucky Juliet and Orly, thought Corrie, getting a whole week of Fa's attention!

It was a week free of responsibility. No one had to worry about the twins at all—about bathing them or feeding them or taking them to and from school. But the next week the twins were fully recovered, Fa went back to his study, and they were on their own once again.

11

Guinevere

Sebastian had barely noticed that the twins had the chicken pox. He became more and more remote, gazing at his sisters and brothers benevolently each morning through half-closed eyelids.

"Are you feeling all right, Sebastian?" Corrie asked him.

His eyes sparkled. "I'm fine!" Corrie waited for him to say more, but he had stopped confiding in her.

He had a secret, she decided. Something was going on in his life—something good, obviously—that had nothing to do with her or the family. So it must have to do with school. Corrie was glad he was happier. But she hated how much he excluded her.

"Let's play a new game," Corrie told Meredith. "Let's spy on Sebastian."

"*Spy* on him! Why?"

Corrie tried to be nonchalant. "Oh, just because he's been acting strange lately. It'll be fun. We can hide somewhere outside his school and wait for him to come out."

The next day they pedalled fast the ten blocks to Laburnum Junior High School. They found some laurel bushes close to the entrance, dragged their bikes into them and collapsed on the damp dirt to catch their breath.

"The bell hasn't even gone yet," panted Corrie. "It's a good thing Sebastian's school gets out later."

They gazed fearfully at the red-brick building. It was so big! Roz said there were more than five hundred students in the whole school. All teenagers, who talked about scary things like dating and make-up and jiving. Corrie felt for Pookie in her jacket pocket. Certainly there would be no place for toy rabbits in grade seven.

"I wish we could stay at our school *forever*," whispered Meredith. They became more and more depressed as the bell rang and swarms of kids holding books congregated on the steps. It was warm for February and the crowd lingered there, mostly in groups of girls and boys eyeing each other. "Hey, Linda!" a boy from one group shouted. "Kevin here says he likes you!" All the girls tittered and all the boys guffawed. White collars and shiny shoes and greased hair sparkled in the winter sun. It was like watching another species.

No wonder Roz abandoned the Round Table! thought Corrie. This school was too real for pretending. And no wonder Sebastian retreated so much into being a knight. You would have to do one or the other—either give in to the teenaged intensity or keep yourself aloof from it. Which would she do?

She was distracted from these confusing thoughts when Meredith hissed, "Look! There's *Roz*!"

Corrie gazed at her pretty sister. She moved down the steps in a pod of her friends. They talked in high, false voices, carefully not looking at the groups of boys. One of the boys, whom Corrie recognized as red-haired Ronnie, stared longingly after Roz. She and her friends disappeared around the corner as they headed for the bike stands.

Most of the groups on the steps had also left. It was chilly under the bushes and Corrie's legs were cramped from squatting in the dirt.

"Maybe Sebastian went out another door," said Meredith.

Then he appeared. He wasn't alone, but was talking to a tall girl with a long thick black braid falling down her back. All her clothes were black too. She had her face turned to his and was listening so avidly that she tripped. Sebastian caught her arm. He kept his hand on it while she went down the rest of the stairs. Then he held her hand while they strolled down the street.

Corrie stood up, her legs shaking.

"Wow!" said Meredith. "He has a *girlfriend!*"

Corrie couldn't answer. What she had just witnessed couldn't be real. She rubbed her freezing hands together as they stood in the sunshine.

"Corrie, are you all right?" Meredith asked her. "*Say* something!"

"It's just so ... odd," said Corrie. "Sebastian's never had a girl-friend before!"

"Well, he *is* fifteen," said Meredith calmly.

"Yes, but ..." She couldn't explain. It was as if her brother had become a stranger. "I know her," she said finally. "She used to go to our school. Her name's Jennifer—Jennifer Layton."

"She looks so *glamorous,* like a movie star!"

"She didn't look like that before. She had shorter hair and she slouched. And she wrote poetry. She made up a poem for Remembrance Day that was so good she had to read it in front of the whole school. She was kind of shy—she kept her head down and mumbled."

"She sure doesn't seem shy *now,*" said Meredith as they got on their bikes.

"I guess people change when they go to junior high," said Corrie. "Like Roz has."

And now, like Sebastian.

CORRIE LONGED TO TELL Sebastian that she knew about Jennifer. But then he would find out she had spied on him. *A knight never lies.* Was it a lie if she just didn't say anything? But if she didn't, how else could she reveal that she knew?

She wrestled with this for several days. Finally, late on Saturday afternoon, she knocked on Sebastian's door. "Will you help me with this hood for Mercury?" she asked.

"You have done an excellent job of this, Gareth," said Sir Lancelot, picking up the tiny hood. "All you need are some ties here."

Corrie stared at her brother, then blurted out, "I know about you and Jennifer."

Sebastian flushed bright red. He motioned Corrie in and closed the door. "You do? How?"

"We—Meredith and I—spied on you," mumbled Corrie. "I'm really sorry, Sebastian," she added quickly as he frowned. "It wasn't honourable. But you've been acting so strange lately and you wouldn't talk to me. I knew you had a secret. I just had to find out!"

"It was wrong of you to spy on me," Sebastian told her. "Knights don't spy on fellow knights. But I'm sorry I was so secretive. I was going to tell you about her sometime. It's just so ... new." He smiled gently.

"Tell me about her now," urged Corrie, sitting on his bed.

"Her name's Jennifer Layton—you probably knew her at Duke of Connaught. Isn't that amazing? 'Jennifer,' like 'Guinevere'! In fact, that's how the name originated—I looked it up."

Now it made sense that Sebastian was suddenly so obsessed with the legends about Guinevere. "Is Jennifer nice?" Corrie asked shyly.

"She's amazing! She writes great poetry. And she doesn't think I'm weird. She really likes my long hair. That's because she's different too. None of the other girls dress or act like her. She's not silly like they are, and she's really confident. She won't do anything that's against her principles. She would make a good knight ... if she wasn't like Guinevere, of course."

"Does she know about the Round Table?"

"Not yet," said Sebastian. "She might think it's too strange."

Corrie was relieved. A knight with a girlfriend was just too confusing.

"The worst thing is that we can't see each other outside of school," said Sebastian. "We walk home every day but I have to leave her a block from her house. Her parents are really strict. She's not allowed to go out with boys until she's sixteen. So we'll have to wait another year before I can take her places."

Corrie felt even more relieved. If Jennifer was only a part of Sebastian's school life, things could stay almost the same.

"You just don't know, Corrie, how incredible Jennifer is. She's perfect. She's exactly like the real Guinevere—beautiful and brave." His face was filled with wonder.

"Guinevere wasn't real, though," said Corrie carefully. "She's just a story. *Jennifer* is the one who's real." And nobody could be that perfect, she thought.

"Well ... they're both real. This is probably hard for you to understand, Corrie, but I think Jennifer is actually a reincarnation of Guinevere."

"A what?"

Sebastian looked excited. "Reincarnation. It's when someone from the past is reborn in someone's body in the present. They come back again. That's what the Round Table is, in a way. I'm the reincarnation of Sir Lancelot. Maybe you're even the reincarnation of Sir Gareth!"

Corrie felt dizzy. The intensity of Sebastian's words, the faraway look in his eyes, scared her. "But Lancelot and Gareth and Guinevere are just stories! They were never real!"

"They *became* stories, but the stories are based on historical figures. There's lots of evidence for that. Someday I'm going to visit Tintagel Castle and Glastonbury in England. Fa's been there. He told me he could actually sense Arthur's presence."

"Okay ... " conceded Corrie. "Maybe King Arthur and his knights *were* real. But I don't see how they can exist again in other people's bodies. That's too weird. Sir Gareth isn't in me. I just *pretend* I'm Sir Gareth."

"It isn't strange at all," said Sebastian patiently. "And probably you aren't a reincarnation of Sir Gareth. You would feel it if you were. Like I do—I *know* Lancelot is in me. Just like I know Guinevere is reincarnated in Jennifer so she and Lancelot can finally be together."

"Does *Jennifer* know? Does she know she's the— What's that word again?"

"Reincarnation."

"Does she know she's the reincarnation of Guinevere?"

Sebastian shook his head. "She's not ready to. One day she'll realize she's Guinevere, but it's not time yet. And I don't want to tell her too soon, in case it scares her."

"*Don't* tell her, Sebastian. She might laugh at you."

"Jennifer? She'd never laugh at me!"

Corrie suddenly felt older than Sebastian. Trying to disguise her worry, she patted his arm and said cheerfully, "Well, I'm glad you have a friend at school. I bet Terry and his gang are nicer to you now."

Sebastian laughed. "Mordred, you mean! He's envious! He likes Jennifer too—he used to follow her around. Like I used to, before she began paying attention to me. She hates Mordred—she told me." He smiled. "I'm glad you know about Jennifer, Corrie. Would you like to meet her sometime?"

"That's okay," said Corrie hastily.

She still wasn't used to the fact that Sebastian was so absorbed in someone outside the family. Actually meeting Jennifer would be too much change. She must be nice, if Sebastian liked her, but Corrie found her threatening.

CORRIE AND ROZ were sitting on Roz's bed while Jingle whizzed around the room. "Why is Sebastian so distracted these days?" asked Corrie. She wanted to hear Roz's version.

"He has a girlfriend!" Roz giggled. "Jennifer Layton—do you remember her from Duke of Connaught? She's kind of strange. She dresses all in black and she wears her hair in a long braid." Her face softened. "But I'm really glad Seb has a girlfriend. He seems much happier, don't you think?"

"Yes ..." said Corrie. What would Roz think if she knew about the reincarnation stuff?

Just the day before, Sebastian had shown Corrie a scarf of Jennifer's that he had tied around his arm under his shirt. He told Corrie it was a "favour," like those that ladies used to give to knights. "It's Guinevere in her that made her give it to me," he said.

"Does she know you've tied it around your arm?"

"No. Jennifer doesn't remember yet that Guinevere used to give favours to Lancelot. She will, though—she's getting more like Guinevere every day."

Corrie had shivered at his words. But Roz made Sebastian sound perfectly normal. Probably there was nothing to worry about. Sebastian was simply in love, and acting as crazy as people in love did in songs and movies. What did *she* know about love? It didn't interest her in the least, so no wonder she couldn't figure out Sebastian.

"Maybe Jennifer will persuade Seb to cut his hair," said Roz. "Maybe he'll even give up the Round Table. Do you still play that?"

"Of course we do! We have meetings every Saturday. Right now we're building a castle on the golf course to be Joyous Gard. And Sebastian will never cut his hair or give up being a knight! He's more Sir Lancelot than he ever was!"

Part of Corrie longed to tell Roz how true and confusing that was now. But if Roz thought there was something wrong with Sebastian, Corrie would have to admit it as well.

Roz smiled at her in an annoyingly grown-up way. "He has to give up the Round Table sometime. He's fifteen! You'll be fine without him—you can be the new head. And soon you'll be too old for it, too. Everyone has to grow up, you know." She gave Corrie a syrupy smile, as if she were the older sister on *Father Knows Best*.

Corrie stood up. "I will *always* be a knight, and so will Sebastian! You don't know what you're missing, Roz, leaving the Round Table!" She held up her head and left the room with as much dignity as she could manage, to cover up the frightened beat of her heart.

12

Merlin

Now Sebastian left the house early, returned just before dinner, and secluded himself in his room all evening. Roz got a part in her school play and sometimes didn't come home until they were all in bed.

On weekdays Corrie became more and more the new head of the family. She drew up the schedule for table setting and baths and dishes, and she continued to tell the younger ones when to go to bed.

Since the only time Sebastian talked to them was at Round Table meetings, Corrie tried to bring up daily problems there. But Sebastian dismissed them. "I have decided that domestic matters have no place at the Round Table," he said when Corrie tried to ask him if the twins' allowance could be raised. He told her she could take the allowance jar out of his room and decide for herself.

But how could she? And how could she know if it was all right for Juliet to go to her friend's house for lunch every day, or where to buy Harry new socks? Juliet was begging for valentines, but Corrie didn't have enough money to buy them.

Corrie tried leaving notes on Roz's pillow. But Roz told her that she was too busy to look after the younger ones. She gave Corrie the clothing money jar and told her to buy Harry some socks and everyone some valentines. "It's your turn to take care of them now," she told Corrie. "I'm tired of it."

"But I'm only eleven!" said Corrie.

Roz smiled. "You're sensible—Aunt Madge always said so. You'll be fine."

That was nice to hear. But worrying about everyone kept Corrie awake. She told Juliet that she had to stay at school for lunch.

"But you go to Meredith's—that's not fair!" said Juliet. Corrie knew she'd go anyway, so after arguing a few more minutes she gave in. At least it was one less sandwich to make.

Corrie rode her bike up to Kerrisdale and bought books of popout valentines for everyone. Shopping for socks, however, seemed so complicated that she raided Sebastian's drawers and found some socks that fit Harry. She decided to raise each person's allowance by five cents. Now the two money jars stared sternly at her from her chest of drawers, like teachers reminding her of her responsibilities.

Just as one group of problems was solved, another came up. The Elephant told Corrie that she would leave unless Hamlet stopped bringing her dead mice. Orly had accidentally broken one of Harry's models; in retaliation Harry had given Orly an Indian burn. A notice came in the mail that the twins were due at the dentist's.

Corrie reminded Harry that knights are kind.

"I'm not a knight yet," said Harry sullenly, "and Orly is a pest. Can't you keep him out of my room?"

Corrie gave him some money to buy a lock. She found mousetraps in the tool room and got Meredith to help her set them.

How she longed to spill out her worries to Meredith! But then her friend might tell her mother and Mrs. Cooper might tell Fa. That would be worst of all, to upset him. The deadline for Fa's book was approaching, and he needed to be left alone. He didn't notice that anything was different, especially because they were still all together on Sundays. Corrie treasured those days more than ever, when the calm routine concealed all the turmoil beneath the surface.

SPRING, AT LEAST, was as predictable and soothing as always. Sentry, Corrie's favourite cherry tree, was coated in fat pink blossoms. The garden was a pastel blur of daffodils and tulips. Corrie's favourites were the grape hyacinths; their tiny bells squeaked when you rubbed them together.

The weather was so warm that Corrie put away her wool skirts. To her surprise, last year's cotton dresses were much too short and tight. She looked in Roz's closet and found two old dresses of hers that fit, one a faded blue and one yellow. Corrie's shoes were too small as well.

She could take some money from the clothing jar to buy new ones, but she was too scared to go downtown on the bus by herself. Then Mrs. Cooper took her and Meredith to the Oakridge Mall. She helped them pick out saddle shoes. Then she tried to buy Meredith a new dress with puffed sleeves. Meredith, however, surprised both her mother and Corrie by asking for a chemise.

"It's too old for you, darling," Mrs. Cooper said.

Corrie stared in horror at the green baggy dress. It looked like a sack! What if her friend was going to start being interested in clothes, like the Five?

"*Please*, Mum," begged Meredith. "I'm *tired* of dressing like a little girl!"

Mrs. Cooper gave in, and Meredith wore her chemise proudly to school the next day. She was the first girl in the school to have one; it liberated her forever from her status as a new girl.

Mr. Zelmach let them play baseball on dry afternoons. Corrie had never had much interest in baseball before. But now she discovered she had a talent for it. If she concentrated, she could hit the ball so hard she often got a home run. It was so exhilarating to dash around the bases while everyone cheered. She was also good at catching the ball with a satisfying *thwack*. She and Meredith practised whenever they could.

"You're so *good*!" said Meredith, who was usually assigned to be a fielder.

"I wish I had my own glove, though," said Corrie. Meredith's was too small for her.

"Why don't you ask your father for one?" suggested Meredith.

Corrie pondered this. It wouldn't be right to take the money out of either of the jars. She had never asked Fa to buy her anything, but why not?

She waited until after dinner. By the time she knocked on Fa's study door and entered the cluttered room she felt tongue-tied with shyness. But Fa's shaggy, kindly expression, as he peered up through his eyebrows from his writing, made her relax.

"Why, Cordelia, how nice to see you!" said Fa, as if they hadn't just had dinner together. "Sit down, my dear. What can I do for you?"

Corrie cleared a pile of papers from a chair and sat facing her father. "I was wondering if you could please give me some money for something I want," she told him.

"And what would that be?"

"A baseball glove. All the kids in my class have them. But I have to share Meredith's."

Fa looked totally confused. "Who is Meredith?"

Corrie began again. She reminded Fa that Meredith was her best friend, realizing with a shock that Fa had never met her. She explained how they were playing baseball almost every day.

Fa smiled. "In my day, it was cricket. Did you know that cricket may go back as far as the Normans? Shepherds played it with matted wads of sheep's wool. Baseball is much newer. It probably started with the English game of rounders ... "

Corrie listened blissfully. Fa really was like Merlin, so full of knowledge. It was wonderful to have his whole attention focused on her. She began telling him about how she hoped to be shortstop next week, but Fa glanced longingly at his manuscript.

"Cordelia, dear, it's delightful to see you, but I must get back to my book."

Corrie had almost forgotten why she came. "Is it all right if I buy a baseball glove, then?" she asked.

"Of course! Go ahead and get one, and I hope you're chosen to be shortstop." Fa picked up his pen and looked down at his manuscript.

"I need some money to get it, though," said Corrie. "I don't want to take it out of the jars, because they're for everyone."

Fa looked up again. "Of course you need money! How stupid of me! How much do you need?"

"The cheapest one I've seen costs a dollar fifty."

Fa pulled out an ancient leather wallet from the jacket hanging over his chair. He stepped carefully around some piles of books on the floor and handed Corrie three dollars. "Don't get the cheapest— get one that will last. That's what your mother always used to say. And keep the change if it's less."

"Thank you, Fa!"

Fa gave her a kiss on her forehead. "You look more and more like your dear mother, you know," he said, perching on the edge of the desk.

"I do?" said Corrie.

"Indeed you do. Tell me, Cordelia, how is the family? Is everything all right? I probably don't pay enough attention to you all."

"You did when the twins were sick," Corrie reminded him.

"So I did, and how utterly exhausting that was! I worry that I'm leaving you with that hard work all the time. Are you sure you can manage?"

How could she begin to tell Fa all her worries? About how strangely Sebastian was acting, how absent Roz was, how uncontrollable the younger ones were, how lonely and difficult it was to be in charge, how much she missed Aunt Madge ...

She couldn't—Fa needed peace to work on his book.

"We're fine," she mumbled.

"Are you sure? Is Sebastian fine? I've noticed he's acting rather oddly these days, as if he's lost in his own world. I worry about Sebastian, you know. He's like Icarus—he flies too close to the sun."

"Icarus?"

"A figure from Greek mythology, my dear." Fa stood up, scanned his packed shelves, and took down a book. "Here, you can read about him. Madge is worried about Sebastian ... that he's still pretending to be a knight. Perhaps he gives himself too wholeheartedly to that game. It was helpful after Molly died—he needed an escape. But Madge thinks Sebastian is avoiding reality." Fa sighed. "I don't know what to think. We all avoid it. 'Human kind cannot bear very much reality,' as Eliot says."

Corrie sighed too. So often she couldn't keep up with Fa's words. But his next ones startled her.

"Madge says I should persuade Sebastian to give up his game."
Fa looked at her much more alertly. "What do you think, Cordelia?
Should I have a talk with him? Not that I think it would do any
good. Sebastian's not going to stop his fantasy just because I ask him
to. Surely it's better to let him grow out of it at his own pace, don't
you agree?"

Corrie wished Fa wasn't speaking to her as if she were older,
when all she wanted to do was sit in his lap the way she used to.

She didn't know what to answer, whether to reassure Fa or to tell
him how scarily Sebastian was now immersed in the game. "I don't
know," she whispered. "You're probably right, though. You can't
stop him pretending." How could she say that Sebastian no longer
seemed to be just pretending?

Yet, if Sebastian stopped the Round Table, they would all
have to. Fa's next words filled her with relief. "I think whatever
Sebastian needs to do, he needs to do. He's always been so sensitive,
so affected by things. 'A perfect gentle knight'—that's what he is."

A perfect gentle knight ... "I like that," said Corrie. "Is it something from a book?"

"It's from Chaucer's *Canterbury Tales.* You'll read that when you
go to university. He wrote it in Old English." Fa went back to his
desk and printed some words on a piece of paper. He handed it to
Corrie, and she smiled at their strangeness: "He was a verray, parfit,
gentil knyght." Fa smiled too. "I have a good translation you would
understand." He stood up again and found a slim book. "You'd like
this—it's full of stories told by a group of pilgrims."

"It sounds really interesting," said Corrie eagerly. She wondered
how long she could prolong this conversation. "Fa," she asked. "Do
you believe in reincarnation?"

Fa chuckled. "What an interesting question! Do *you*?"

"I don't know. Someone I know does, though."

Fa looked wistful. "I'd like to believe that people come back after they die. Perhaps they do when a relative is like them—the way you remind me of my mother sometimes."

"That's what Aunt Madge says. But you just said I was like Mum!"

"You look like Molly. But your character is more like your grandmother's. Juliet is more like Molly, with her impetuous nature. But no, Cordelia, I don't personally believe that someone can be reborn as another person. Unfortunately, when someone is gone she is gone."

Was he going to cry? No. The pain on Fa's face changed into a smile. "Lots of people—indeed, whole religions—do believe in reincarnation. There are many books about it."

"If lots of people believe in it does that mean reincarnation is real, or does it just mean that the person who *believes* it thinks it's real?"

"You're getting to be quite a philosopher, Cordelia! Reincarnation is real in the sense that religion is real. It's just not real for everyone, the way the sun rising is real. Does that help?"

"Sort of."

"Good. Here, I'll lend you a book about Eastern religions and you can read about it." He picked out another book and Corrie added it to her pile.

Reading about things was always Fa's answer to difficult questions. She supposed it helped, but she wished he could just give her the answers right now.

But Fa turned back to his desk for good. "It's been delightful visiting with you, Cordelia. Now I really must get back to work. But come again—we don't talk enough, you and I. And you'll tell me if anything is wrong, won't you? Promise?"

Corrie grinned. "I promise."

She slipped out of the study, feeling lighter than when she went in. And she was going to get a baseball glove!

THAT NIGHT CORRIE STRUGGLED through some of the book on reincarnation. Then she gazed out at the moon and thought as hard as she could.

She could see what a comforting belief reincarnation was. She could even see that it was possible, the way it was possible that Jesus or Buddha had existed. It was truer than pretending, truer than Santa Claus or the Round Table. Those were *just* pretending.

When she pretended she was Sir Gareth it seemed true for the time she was playing. But she wasn't Sir Gareth every moment of the day and she definitely wasn't the reincarnation of Sir Gareth.

Was Sir Lancelot reborn in Sebastian? Was Jennifer really Guinevere? Definitely not, Corrie decided. Perhaps Sebastian really did believe in reincarnation. That was fine. It was the same thing as saying the Creed in church.

Corrie thought even harder. If reincarnation were true, people who had died probably couldn't plan it. That was the trouble with Sebastian thinking he was Sir Lancelot and Jennifer was Guinevere. He wanted that, so he believed it. But it was too tidy, too coincidental that Lancelot and Guinevere would come back as teenagers at the same school.

Corrie's brain was spinning so fast that after she was in bed, she made a mental list to sort out her thoughts.

1. Reincarnation could be possible. How could she argue with what millions of people believed in? It was such an appealing idea that perhaps she would come to believe in it herself one day.

2. However, Sebastian was not the reincarnation of Sir Lancelot, and Jennifer was not Guinevere. That was Sebastian's fantasy, an extension of the fantasy he'd had for years of being a knight. If he told himself it was reincarnation it helped make his fantasy real.

3. This was the hardest: Was this good for Sebastian? Corrie didn't know. She wanted him to be happy. It was normal for teenagers to be in love, and Sebastian needed an ally at school. Perhaps as long as he didn't tell Jennifer, it would be okay for him to pretend what he did.

Corrie couldn't think about it any longer. It was too hard. She fell asleep trying to decide what kind of baseball glove she would buy.

MEREDITH ASKED HER FATHER to take them to a sporting goods store. Corrie picked out a beautiful new glove. It was golden leather and it had a rich earthy smell. The next day she was picked to be shortstop. She was sure her new glove had brought her luck, because she caught the ball every time.

After the game they all sprawled on the grass while Mr. Zelmach read them a poem called "Casey at the Bat."

Jamie was sitting next to Corrie. "You did great, Corrie," he whispered.

Corrie smiled at him with surprise. The sun warmed the top of her head, and the white patches of her new saddle shoes gleamed. Spring was really here, and everything seemed possible again.

13

Jennifer

To Corrie's relief, Sebastian offered to take the twins to the dentist. "Why don't you come too?" he asked her.

Corrie agreed eagerly. All the way there, the four of them pretended the bus was a dragon. It certainly sounded like one as it hissed its way over the bridge.

The twins pressed into Sebastian's side and pulled on his arms. They had missed him as much as she did, Corrie realized.

"Did any of the knights kill dragons?" Orly asked.

"*Slay*," said Juliet. "Knights slayed dragons, right, Sebastian?"

"You are right, Master Jules," said Sir Lancelot, "but the word is 'slew,' not 'slayed.' Sir Tristan slew a dragon and cut out its tongue," he told Orly.

"Neat!" said Orly. "Can I be Sir Tristan when I'm knighted?"

"We'll see."

"*I* want to be Sir Tristan!" said Juliet.

Orly pulled her hair. "You can't! I thought of it first!"

"Neither of you will ever be knighted unless you stop arguing," Sebastian said calmly.

Corrie melted into the relief of having him take charge again.

Orly was ushered in to the dentist first. Corrie listened to Juliet proudly sound out words from a magazine; she'd been reading fluently for a month now, the first one in her class to do so. Then Juliet went in to get her teeth cleaned. Corrie showed Sebastian a picture of a knight in an ad.

"They've left out his besagews," said Sebastian.

"What are besagews?" asked Corrie happily. Sebastian was so much more *present* today. Maybe his aloofness was over.

Just as Sebastian began to explain, the door opened and a dark-haired girl walked in. He jumped up. "Jenny!"

"Hi, Seb," said Jennifer. "So we share the same dentist!"

"Um ... this is my sister Corrie," muttered Sebastian. His words tumbled over one another, and when he sat down again he kept pulling at his shirt.

"Hi." Jennifer smiled. At least, her mouth smiled. Her greenish-grey eyes narrowed coldly as she looked at Corrie.

She doesn't like me, thought Corrie. She realized instantly that she didn't like Jennifer either.

She looks like a ... a snake, she decided, like the long snake of her dark braid. A slithery snake that was entwining herself around her brother. Jennifer sat down beside Sebastian, much too close. Corrie had had her brother's entire attention just minutes ago. Now he ignored her.

"Do you have a sore tooth, Sebbie?"

Sebbie! Corrie glared at her.

"No, it's just the twins who have to be here. We're waiting for them. How about you?" Sebastian's face grew gentle.

"Oh, I'm just here for a check-up." Sebastian gazed at her as if these ordinary words were poetry.

"What grade are you in, Corrie?" Jennifer asked. She wasn't really interested; she was just asking to please Sebastian.

"Six," mumbled Corrie.

Jennifer hadn't even heard. She turned back to Sebastian. The two of them acted as if Corrie wasn't in the room.

Orly pranced out with a pinwheel in his hand. "No cavities!" he boasted. He stared at Jennifer. "Who are you?"

"This is Jennifer," Sebastian told him.

"And you must be Seb's little brother! I've heard great things about you. Can I try your pinwheel?" gushed Jennifer. She blew on it and Orly grinned.

The nurse ushered Jennifer in. She pressed Sebastian's hand and left. Both he and Orly gazed after her as if they were bewitched.

Juliet appeared with another pinwheel. With relief, Corrie turned to go. But Sebastian hesitated. "Corrie, do you think you could take the twins home by yourself? I'm going to wait for Jennifer."

"But I've never gone on the bus by myself!"

"You'll be fine. I'll take you to the bus stop. Look for number twenty—it goes straight down Granville. All you have to do is get off at the street opposite the church."

Corrie was torn. It would be an adventure taking the bus, but she didn't want to leave Sebastian alone with that girl. Still, what difference did it make? They saw each other every day anyway.

"Jennifer is really pretty!" said Orly after they had gone down in the elevator.

"Who's Jennifer?" demanded Juliet.

"She's Sebastian's girlfriend, right?" asked Orly.

Juliet gawked at Sebastian. "You have a *girlfriend*?"

"Yes, I do," said Sebastian softly. "And do you know what, Juliet and Orly? She's really Guinevere!"

The twins looked at him with surprised round eyes. "She is?"

"Yes! Jennifer is the reincarnation of Guinevere."

"Re-what?"

"Reincarnation. I'll explain it to you later."

When they reached the bus stop, Sebastian gave Corrie some money. "See you later!" he called, walking rapidly back towards the building.

Corrie stood at the bus stop trying to concentrate on watching for number twenty. The twins helped her and crowed, "There it is!" when it appeared. They mounted the stairs and Corrie carefully deposited the money in the coin box. She found them a seat near the back. People smiled at them and she felt proud to be responsible enough to take her little sister and brother on the bus all by herself.

When they got comfortable, and when Orly and Juliet were absorbed in looking out the window, she finally let herself think about Jennifer.

She hated her. She hated the way she sucked up to Sebastian, pretending to be nice to Orly just so he would approve. She was dangerous, a dangerous black snake who had cast a spell over her brother. Most of all, she hated the way Sebastian had paid more attention to her than to Corrie—his favourite sister!

Corrie was so full of anguish she didn't even feel proud when they approached the church and she pulled the string in time for their stop.

"Do you know what that 're' word means?" Juliet asked her as they walked down the street.

Corrie gave a short explanation about reincarnation. "So Sebastian thinks that the Guinevere from the King Arthur stories is alive again in Jennifer's body," she finished.

"Cool!" said Orly.

"Does that mean that Sir Lancelot has come back again as Sebastian?" asked Juliet.

"No!" Corrie shouted, so loud that they stopped and stared at her. "Listen to me, you guys," she continued. "Sebastian being Lancelot and Jennifer being Guinevere, all of the Round Table, is just *pretending.* It's not real! Sebastian isn't really Sir Lancelot and Jennifer sure isn't Guinevere. I'm not Sir Gareth and you're not really pages."

"We are so!" yelled Orly.

"You're fibbing, Corrie," said Juliet. "Me and Orly are pages and soon we'll be squires and then we'll be knights. I'll be Sir Tristan and Orly will be Sir Bors or someone else. And Sebastian *is* Sir Lancelot!"

"And Jennifer is Guinevere!" said Orly firmly. "She's beautiful, just like Guinevere in the stories. Anyway, Sebastian said so!"

"You're fibbing!" cried Juliet again.

"I'm sorry," Corrie told them. "You'll understand when you get older." The twins glared at her, then ran ahead down the street.

Corrie followed slowly, not wanting to believe her own words. When *she* was six, she had spent months being Pookie. No one in the family had guessed that she had wings and flew all over the world having adventures. She hadn't *pretended* she was Pookie—she *was* Pookie.

That complete immersion in another world had gone. Now Corrie was more and more aware of only pretending; she was gradually losing a magic she could never get back.

I don't *want* to lose it! thought Corrie. But the sensible part of her knew she had to. Did Sebastian?

CORRIE KNOCKED ON Sebastian's door later that evening.

"Can I talk to you?" she asked.

"Of course! Wasn't it great to run into Jennifer like that? Did you like her?"

What could she say? He would be so disappointed if she told him the truth. "She's okay," mumbled Corrie. "I don't think she likes *me*, though."

"Of course she does! I talk about you a lot—she knows how close we are."

Maybe that was why Jennifer didn't like her. Maybe she didn't want to share Sebastian any more than Corrie did.

There was nothing she could do about her and Jennifer. Corrie was more worried about Sebastian. "Do you *really* think Jennifer is the reincarnation of Guinevere?" she asked him.

That intense look came into her brother's eyes. "It sounds strange, but, yes, I really do! I've felt that ever since the first time I talked to her. We were meant to be together—we're soul mates."

"Because ... because you're really Sir Lancelot?" whispered Corrie.

Sebastian nodded solemnly. "I know you probably think I'm crazy, but why else have I felt so drawn to him all these years? And why else would I keep on with the Round Table? I hate to admit it, but Roz is right. It's fine to play at knights when you're your age, but fifteen is too old for it. Except I'm not playing! The rest of you are—it's just a game for you. But for me, it's real. I have no choice."

"But Sebastian ... " What could she possibly say? She spoke slowly and carefully, as if she were trying to explain something to Orly. "Sebastian, listen to me. I don't agree with you. I read about reincarnation, and maybe it can happen. But I don't think it's happened with you. You aren't Lancelot and Jennifer isn't Guinevere. It's not good for you to believe that."

Sebastian smiled at her. "It's hard to understand. You don't have to believe me, but it's true. And I'm fine—I've never felt this happy."

"But that's because you're in love!" blurted out Corrie. "Everyone feels happy when they're in love—at least that's what all the songs and movies say."

Sebastian laughed. "I *am* in love! But it's more than that. I'm growing into my true self, and so is Jennifer."

"But what will happen? How can you be Lancelot and Guinevere *now*, in 1958?"

Sebastian shrugged calmly. "I don't know what will happen. Our true selves will let us know." He swivelled his chair back to his desk. "Now, Gareth, I have lots of studying to do, so you had better go. Pray do not worry yourself about me."

Corrie left the room quickly. She ran to her room, closed the door, and huddled on the windowseat. The trees below her swayed in the wind. It blew through the crack in her window and she got her eiderdown, pulling it tightly around her to stop shivering.

Sebastian seemed to truly believe that he was Sir Lancelot and Jennifer was Guinevere. Should she tell Fa? But what could he do? He might just repeat that Sebastian was that Icarus person and that he had to grow out of his fantasy at his own pace.

Perhaps it would be all right. Sebastian would soon tell Jennifer about his convictions and Jennifer would laugh at him—Corrie could hear her cackle like a witch. And then they would break up. Sebastian would be miserable, but he'd recover. Corrie could comfort him.

And then Sebastian would also get over his strange beliefs. Everything would be like it was before: they would carry on being knights, but Sebastian would just be pretending, as he used to.

Corrie got ready for bed, picked up Pookie, and snuggled into her pillow. She tried being Sir Gareth, lying on his pallet in the great hall of Camelot after the nightly feast, his loyal greyhound at his side and his sword close at hand.

"Hark!" Sir Gareth whispered to Sir Perceval. "Do you hear something stirring outside the castle walls?" She imagined the two of them creeping out into the moonlight and encountering a rival knight trying to sneak in. They drew their swords and the knight bolted.

A part of her was observing, watching herself pretend. But at least some of the magic was still there.

14

Robin Hood and Little John

$\mathcal{M}$rs. Cooper invited the whole Bell family for Easter dinner. When Corrie asked Fa he said, "Please thank her, my dear, but you know we always go to the Hotel Vancouver for Easter."

Corrie was relieved. She couldn't imagine mixing up her family and Meredith's. What would Fa and the Coopers talk about? They had nothing in common. Mr. Cooper had told her, when he heard what Fa taught, how boring he had found Shakespeare in school.

The Easter Bunny left his usual large basket of chocolate treats in the hall. Hamlet ate a foil-covered egg and threw it up on Harry's bed. Corrie felt queasy herself after nibbling both ears of her rabbit.

"If *only* you could come for dinner!" Meredith told her after church.

Now Corrie wished Fa had been more sociable. She vaguely remembered how the house used to hum with Fa and Mum's friends, friends who talked avidly about books and art, and whom she could hear laughing and dancing long after she had gone to bed. Fa had not invited anyone over since Mum's death. All he had were his books, his teaching, and his family.

Harry and Fa spent most of Easter dinner discussing the huge explosion that had happened near Vancouver the day before, when Ripple Rock had been blown up.

"It's the biggest non-atomic blast in history!" Harry said proudly.

"But why did they blow it up?" Juliet asked. Fa explained how the underwater mountain had caused many shipping accidents over the years.

Roz was patiently listening to Orly's riddles, and Sebastian was daydreaming as usual. Corrie poked at her overdone roast beef. She wondered what the Coopers were having.

During the Easter holidays Sebastian called a meeting of the Round Table every day. They met at Joyous Gard, which was now finished—a spacious fort of woven branches with a canvas roof and a blanket for a door. From the clearing you couldn't even tell it was there.

Building the fort had been fun, but now that it was done they had to sit for long periods in Joyous Gard while Sebastian read to them. Corrie tried to pay attention, but it was so hard to be shut out from the sun in this shadowy space. The others were also restless.

"Can't we have a sword fight?" Juliet asked.

"Maybe later, Master Jules. Now listen carefully to the story of how Sir Lancelot rescued Guinevere."

No one could listen. It was as if Sebastian were reading to himself.

"What is wrong with all of you?" he scolded, when the younger ones started pinching each other. "You are not paying attention!"

Corrie saw how white his face was. "We are trying to, sire," she said. "But it is a long time for the squire and the pages to sit still."

Sebastian sighed. "Very well, you may all go and joust." The others rushed out and Corrie tried to smile at her brother. But Sebastian had bent over the book again.

NOW CORRIE'S ONLY SOLACE was Meredith's friendship. After the holidays were over she started seeing Meredith on Saturdays as well as on weekdays, walking to the Coopers' house as soon as the Round Table meeting ended.

The first Saturday, Mrs. Cooper took Meredith and Corrie downtown to have lunch at the Georgia Hotel. They had vanilla milkshakes and two chocolate eclairs each. After lunch they went to the art gallery and gazed at paintings by Emily Carr. Corrie liked how the dark tree forms invited her right into the pictures.

Mrs. Cooper dropped them off at the Orpheum to see *Old Yeller*. When she picked them up afterwards, Meredith was in floods of tears.

"I will never, *ever* go to another movie again," she sobbed. "That was *awful*! The poor, poor dog!"

"Darling, it was just a story!" said Mrs. Cooper. But Meredith cried all the way home in the car. "Why is she always like this with movies?" her mother asked Corrie. "*You* seem to have survived it. Can you explain to Meredith what's real and what isn't?"

Corrie shook her head. If only she could ... especially to Sebastian.

THE NEXT SATURDAY Corrie put on her blue dress, plus an old straw hat of Mum's she had found in a closet, because Meredith wanted to play "Anne of Green Gables."

Meredith was Diana. She was obviously relishing her role, telling Corrie how glad she was that the two of them were "bosom friends." She poured real tea into the cups and saucers she had set up on a table in the back yard. Paisley, enjoying the sunshine in his cage, practised saying "Hello there" endlessly. Meredith picked up the sugar tongs. "One or two lumps?" she asked in a mincing voice

"Two, please," muttered Corrie. She couldn't get involved in this stupid game. It was so boring—there was nothing to it. At least Mrs. Cooper's cookies were as delicious as usual. She brought them out more tea and complimented them on their hats. Then she told Meredith she and Mr. Cooper were going out for a few hours.

"Let's play another game now," Corrie suggested.

Meredith looked disappointed. "Don't you want to keep having tea? I know, we could make some Kool-Aid and pretend it's rasp-berry cordial. Then I could get *drunk,* like Diana does in the book!"

"Can't we play Robin Hood?"

Meredith shrugged. "I guess so." They put the tea things back in the kitchen and went upstairs to change. Meredith lent Corrie a pair of shorts and a T-shirt. Corrie was worried. Why was Meredith suddenly so reluctant about playing Robin Hood? She had been totally absorbed when they had started this new game a few weeks ago. Corrie had given plenty of time to Meredith's silly tea; shouldn't she have a turn now?

Back in the yard, they tidied up the fort they had made behind the garage and picked up the bows they had made out of branches and string. They had glued Paisley's discarded feathers to the bamboo arrows; the tips were covered with points modelled out of Plasticine.

Corrie was Robin Hood. "Well, Little John, are you ready to track down the sheriff's men?" she asked.

To her relief, Meredith answered properly. "Yes, Robin. I think I saw some tracks under the greenwood tree."

The sun beat down. "It's so *hot*—let's take off our tops!" suggested Meredith.

Corrie felt shy. But after Meredith had stripped off her T-shirt, she did the same. They glanced at each other. Corrie was flatter than Meredith, but both were starting to develop. At least neither was ready for a bra yet, thought Corrie. Only one girl in their class, Sharon, had a bra—she had boasted about it for a whole day.

Corrie slung a quiver over her shoulder and came out of the fort. It was delightful to feel the sun all over her bare top. She poked her friend. "John—can you hear voices? Let's spy on them."

Clutching their bows, the outlaws crept up to the fence and peeked through knotholes at Meredith's neighbours. A woman was weeding with her back to them, and her teenaged son was talking to her. He was trying to persuade her to let him use the car.

"An arrow would go through here," whispered Corrie. She fitted an arrow into her bow and poked it into the hole.

"You wouldn't *really*!" giggled Meredith.

"Of course not. But look how easy it would be." Corrie drew the string as taut as she could and aimed the arrow at the head of the young man.

"I know this man, John. It's the sheriff of Nottingham himself! If I aim carefully I can finish him off, the dastard."

"*Do* it, Robin! It would be a brave deed, and all the poor people would thank you for it."

Corrie didn't mean to let her arrow go. She really didn't. But somehow, Meredith's words had fuzzed the line between what was real and what was pretending. And somehow the arrow flew through the hole.

There was a loud, horrible screech.

"Oh, *no*! Corrie, what have you *done*!"

Corrie sank to the ground, choking with fear. Had she killed him? Would she go to jail?

"What's going on here?" A very red and angry face appeared over the fence. "Do you realize you've just hit my cat?"

The girls stood up. "I'm awfully *s-sorry*, Mrs. Patrick," stuttered Meredith. "It was just a game. Is Boodles all *right*?"

"I don't know yet—he's taken off into the bushes and Malcolm can't get him to come out." The woman glared at them. "What do you think you're doing, Meredith Cooper, shooting arrows through fences? Are your parents home?"

"They're out," whispered Meredith.

"Well, when they get back they are certainly going to hear about this. Running around half-naked, injuring poor little cats ... You're a pair of hooligans!"

"We're really, really sorry," gulped Corrie, but Mrs. Patrick had stomped off.

Corrie and Meredith ran into the house. Meredith put on a T-shirt and Corrie got into her dress again. Then they peeked from behind the curtains in Mr. and Mrs. Cooper's bedroom and tried to see if the cat was all right. Malcolm was still calling him, a tin of cat food in his hand. Finally a large ginger-and-white cat ambled out of the shrubs. Malcolm picked him up and went into the house.

"He looks okay," said Corrie. "Oh, Meredith, what if I hurt him?" She felt like throwing up.

"But why did you let go of your *arrow*?" Meredith asked, her face ashen.

"I don't know," said Corrie miserably. "You said do it and I just ... I just did."

"But you *know* I didn't mean to *really* shoot!"

"I know. But I ... forgot, I guess." Corrie hung her head.

Meredith sat beside her, patting her back awkwardly. She grimaced. "Mum and Dad are going to be *really* mad."

They were sitting glumly in the kitchen drinking Kool-Aid when Meredith's parents arrived home.

"Why such long faces?" asked Mr. Cooper, chucking Meredith under the chin. Meredith couldn't answer. He kissed the top of her head and took out the garbage. Then the phone rang.

Corrie and Meredith stared at the floor while Mrs. Cooper listened to the angry voice coming out of the receiver. Her pretty face grew more and more astonished. "They *what*? Is he all right? Yes, I agree ... I'll talk to them ... All right ... Goodbye."

She hung up the phone and called Meredith's father back into the kitchen. Then they all sat down. "That was Mrs. Patrick, girls," she said quietly. "Can you tell me what happened?"

Corrie and Meredith stumbled out their tale. By the time they finished Meredith was sobbing.

"Do you realize how dangerous it is to play with weapons?" Mr. Cooper said seriously. "You could have hit a person, not a cat!"

"Is the cat all right?" whispered Corrie.

"Yes, the cat is apparently fine," said Meredith's mother, "but you are very lucky he is."

"You are never to play that game again, Meredith and Corrie," Mr. Cooper told them sternly. "I want to see you break all your bows and arrows, all right?"

They nodded.

"You're far too old to be playing boys' games anyhow," said Mrs. Cooper. "What happened to your nice tea party? And Mrs. Patrick said you had taken off your T-shirts! You can't do that any more, you know—you're both growing into young ladies."

They had to go next door and apologize. Mrs. Patrick hadn't softened. She stood in her doorway and ranted at them for an eternity while they stood there with hanging heads. Her brittle words were like sharp pebbles she was pouring over them.

As Corrie trudged home, Mrs. Cooper's soft words rankled just as much. "Young ladies"—yech! Silly teenagers, like Roz and Jennifer. She was never going to be like that!

But now a whole private game had been banned. It was all her fault, of course, but she still felt betrayed, as if the grown-ups had made them break far more than their bows and arrows.

15

"Out of His Wit"

As the long, slow spring grew greener and more fragrant, Corrie's world became grey. Meredith suddenly no longer wanted to pretend anything.

"I know we can't be Robin Hood and Little John, but why don't we pretend we're in the Narnia books?" argued Corrie. "Or we could play with the animals again."

But Meredith only wanted to play catch, or roller skate or explore on their bikes. All of these things were fun, but they weren't magic. Meredith was just as nice a friend as ever—but she was just Meredith, not Sir Perceval or Raccy or Edward.

Home was worse. Something was wrong with Sebastian. Now he went straight to his room after school, appearing for meals and secluding himself again right after them. He spoke only when he was answering a question and then it was in a stifled voice, as if he could barely form the words. He didn't even call meetings of the Round Table.

Corrie tried to assemble everyone one Saturday morning, but the meeting seemed thin and boring without Sebastian there. "Because of Sir Lancelot's absence, we will cancel Round Table meetings for the time being," she told them.

"But we'll have another one soon, right?" asked Harry anxiously.

Corrie tried to smile at him. "Of course we will. We're just taking a break until Sir Lancelot returns."

Juliet looked confused. "But Sir Lancelot is here! He's in his room!"

"As a knight he's not here," Corrie explained. "He's ... he's off on a quest, on a quest for the Holy Grail. Let's pretend we're with him on the quest. That's why we won't meet in Camelot or Joyous Gard for a while."

By the next day, the younger ones seemed to have forgotten they were ever knights. Orly and Juliet became cowboys, and Harry began going to his friend Peter's every day after school when he was free of the twins.

Corrie wandered around the house as if she were lost in it. She tried to be Sir Gareth on her own, but Sir Gareth was as lost as Sir Lancelot. All she could do was read. At least in books she could still escape into another world. Every day she wasn't at Meredith's she lay on her bed and found solace in a novel.

She couldn't escape from Sebastian's miserable, tense face, however. One afternoon she knocked on his door and asked him if anything was wrong.

"Nothing's wrong," he mumbled.

"Why aren't we having the Round Table any more?"

"I haven't got time," said Sebastian. "I have too much homework."

He wasn't doing homework, though. Corrie was glad to see he was reading *The Boy's King Arthur*.

"How's Jennifer?" she made herself ask.

"I wot not how Guinevere is," Sebastian said dully. His tragic voice made Corrie wince.

So that was it—they must have "broken up," as Roz would call it. She forgot how much she had wanted this. Sebastian was so anguished, Corrie now wished it hadn't happened.

"Did you ... did you tell Jennifer about her being Guinevere and you being Sir Lancelot?" she whispered.

"That I did," said Sebastian. "But she was not ready to know it. I told her too soon and she did not believe me."

Corrie wondered if Jennifer had mocked Sebastian. "Do *you* still believe it?" she asked him.

Sebastian turned back to his desk. "Would you please go, Corrie? I have a lot to do."

Corrie sat on the hall stairs, trying to think clearly. When Sebastian had been with Jennifer he'd been strange, but happy. Now he was just strange—and so distant, as if she were neither his sister nor his fellow knight. He had never seemed this far away.

The sun coming through the bevelled windows made soft prisms on the carpet and walls. When Corrie was little she had thought the stripes of light were fairies. Hamlet slept peacefully on the landing, his fur dotted with colour. Corrie envied his utter oblivion.

She had to find out what had happened. Roz was home for dinner that night, and while they were doing the dishes Corrie asked her if Sebastian and Jennifer had stopped seeing each other.

"It looks like it. She's going out with Terry, of all people! How could she stand him?"

"Terry! Oh, poor Sebastian! Roz, I think there's something wrong with him. He won't talk to me, and he spends all his time in his room. He doesn't tell us what to do any more."

Roz shrugged. "So what else is new? He's been like that for ages, ever since he started going out with Jennifer."

"But now we don't even have Round Table meetings!"

"Sebastian will be okay. He'll get over it. And I'm glad he's finally stopped that game. It wasn't good for him—it wasn't good for any of us. *I'm* in love now, Corrie, with Ronnie! Do you want me to tell you how it started?"

"No!" Corrie strode out of the kitchen. Roz was hopeless. And Corrie had a dreadful feeling that Sebastian wouldn't "get over it." Instead he seemed to be sinking into a place where no one could reach him.

THEN SEBASTIAN STOPPED coming home after school. They had all become so used to him hiding in his room that at first no one noticed he wasn't even in the house. Sometimes Harry or Juliet or Orly would ask where he was. Roz didn't seem to care, and she was often out herself, anyway. Sebastian would turn up for dinner, eat silently, then retreat to his room. It was just like when he was in love, but now he was silent and miserable instead of in a happy daze.

The twins got wilder and wilder. Orly broke a window at school and Juliet bit a boy in her class. Corrie had no control over them, and they were becoming dirtier and ruder every day. All three of the younger kids ignored Corrie's orders to go to bed. Harry refused to take his turn with the twins after school and spent all his time at Peter's—they were making a rocket, he told Corrie.

Meredith kept asking Corrie to come over, but she started to say no most days, and she discouraged Meredith from coming to her house. She didn't have the heart or strength to do anything but try to hold her disintegrating family together.

She tried to make a schedule for June, but it was so difficult when Sebastian and Roz weren't home to do things. Harry ignored

her when she begged him to take out the garbage, and Juliet stuck
her tongue out when Corrie asked her to dry the dishes. "You aren't
my boss!" she called, scampering up the stairs. Most nights Corrie
had to do all the meals and cleaning up herself, with a little help
from Orly when she bribed him with bubble gum.

Fa, of course, didn't even notice. He told them his book was
almost ready to be sent to the typist. Now that classes were over at
the university, he was retreating to his study whenever he could.
They had his full attention only on Sundays.

CORRIE FELT SO HELPLESS that she devised a plan. She would spy
on Sebastian again and find out what he was doing after school.
A knight is loyal. She had to try to keep on being Sir Gareth, to be
loyal to Sir Lancelot and not give up on him.

The next day she forced Harry to take the twins home by riding
away from him on her bike. She pedalled fast to Laburnum school
and hid behind the same shrubs she had with Meredith.

The first people she recognized were Jennifer and Terry. Jennifer
was laughing that same false laugh she had used with Sebastian. She
had cut off her braid and now she wore make-up. Her sweater
stretched tightly over her pointy bra—she looked like a teenager in
a magazine. Terry couldn't keep his eyes off her. His friends looked
at her just as avidly.

The two of them were so disgusting they deserved each other,
Corrie decided. No matter how unhappy Sebastian was, at least
Jennifer was out of his life.

Roz appeared with Joyce and they quickly walked away, deep in
conversation. At least Roz wasn't with Ronnie.

Finally Sebastian emerged. He pushed through the crowd and
everyone parted, as if he were a plague. Even Terry and his gang
ignored him—they were too enthralled by Jennifer.

Sebastian mounted his bike and Corrie followed. He rode towards Kerrisdale. Corrie swerved in and out of cars, panting with concentration. It was so difficult to stay close to the side of the street.

Finally Sebastian drew up in front of the Kerrisdale library. Corrie locked up her bike and followed him in.

Hiding behind a stack of books, she got back her breath. She found her brother sitting at a table in the adult non-fiction section. He was surrounded by stacks of books, his hand on his forehead while he leaned over one.

Corrie watched him for a long time. Sebastian looked exhausted. There were deep circles under his eyes. His hair was unwashed and hung greasily behind his ears. His fingernails were lined with dirt. He turned a page and sighed, then looked up. Corrie drew back quickly. She could still see his face. It was so full of pain that she felt as if she'd been stabbed.

Sebastian got up and she saw him go into the men's washroom. Darting over to the table, she glanced at the books and then flew back to her hiding place.

Knights and King Arthur ... Books by Malory and Tennyson and Pyle. The book he was reading was open to a page depicting a drawing by Howard Pyle labelled "The Lady Guinevere." Corrie had only a few seconds to notice how much her snooty expression resembled Jennifer's.

Corrie slipped out of the library, got on her bike, and rode slowly home. Sebastian seemed to be just as obsessed with Guinevere as he had been before, even though Jennifer was now out of his life. Did he still think he was the reincarnation of Sir Lancelot?

That night Corrie re-read the story of how, when Guinevere was angry at Lancelot, he became "out of his wit," existing for two years on fruit and water and running around half-naked. Was Sebastian going as mad as Lancelot?

Sebastian continued to stay away until dinnertime, but at least Corrie now knew where he was.

"Seb, how long has it been since you've washed?" Roz asked one weekend. "Your hair and clothes are disgusting, and you stink!"

"Mind your own business," he muttered, and went upstairs.

"He's as bad as Orly!" Roz complained to Corrie. "What's wrong with him?"

"Something *is* wrong with him!" said Corrie. "I think we should tell Fa."

"Don't bother him—you know how hard he's working these days." Roz looked exasperated. "I guess Sebastian is still upset over Jennifer, but he's acting like a child. I'll talk to him."

"He won't listen to you," warned Corrie. She watched Roz go up the stairs. A door slammed and Roz came down almost immediately.

"He's impossible! He won't even let me in his room!"

"I told you," said Corrie sadly. "It's as if he isn't here."

"Well, I'm fed up with him. He doesn't do anything to help any more."

"Roz, neither do you!" cried Corrie. "I've been doing *everything*!"

Roz flushed. "I'm sorry, Corrie. You're absolutely right. I tell you what, once the play is over next week, I'll come straight home from school every day until Sebastian's better."

"Thanks. But, Roz—do we just wait? Do you think Sebastian *will* get better? I still think we should tell Fa."

"No! We'll just wait. If Seb's going to be so stubborn, we'll ignore him. After a while he'll be ashamed of how he's acting."

"I don't think he's acting this way on purpose," Corrie said. "It's as if he can't help it."

"Of course he can help it! He's just feeling sorry for himself."

Corrie shook her head. "He's not. It's as if he's under some sort of spell. He's still Sir Lancelot, you know. Except he's not pretending any more—it's as if he really *is* Sir Lancelot."

Roz stood up angrily. "Of course he's not! I'm so tired of hearing about that stupid game! It's about time you all gave it up, especially Sebastian!"

Corrie's voice broke. "We *have* given it up—*except* for Sebastian!"

"Well, he just has to grow up. Until he does, we'll have to cope without bothering Fa. Don't you dare tell him, promise?"

Corrie nodded, tears blurring her vision. She blinked them away and went upstairs to start another comforting diorama.

Roz and Corrie got the household onto a fragile schedule again. The twins didn't listen to them as they did to Sebastian, but they were slightly more obedient. The dishes got done and bedtimes were re-established.

But Sebastian became worse. He hardly ate at meals but nibbled on peanut butter and crackers in between. His skin broke out into ugly inflamed pimples. His teeth were furry—Corrie was sure he never brushed them. He was losing so much weight that his clothes hung loosely and his cheeks became hollow. Every time Roz nagged at him he snarled at her so violently that she finally gave-up. "Okay, be filthy—see if I care!"

Corrie tried to talk to him too, but he was gently dismissive. "I'm okay," he said. "I just want to be left alone, all right?"

"Don't they notice at school how dirty he is?" Corrie asked Roz.

"I don't know. Maybe not—all the boys have greasy hair. They put stuff in it to make it even greasier. And teachers never really notice you."

Roz was right. Mr. Zelmach, nice as he was, didn't see how unhappy Corrie was.

Lately she had hardly even spoken to or played with Meredith. When Meredith tried to ask her why, Corrie dismissed her friend the same way Sebastian had dismissed her. It was as if whatever was ailing Sebastian was catching.

Corrie read the story of Sir Lancelot being "out of his wit" over and over. All that saved him was lying next to the Holy Grail. Corrie felt out of her own wit. She had no Holy Grail to heal her brother, and anyway, that was just a story. This was real, but as Fa had said, it was too much reality to bear.

16

A Knight Is Brave

"But why can't I come to *your* house?" asked Meredith. For the umpteenth time Corrie had just explained that she couldn't go to Meredith's because she had to be at home. Whenever she saw Meredith these days she felt split in two. Part of her wished Meredith would leave her alone, but part of her was glad that her friend was staying loyal.

"It's too complicated," Corrie sighed. "You just can't come, that's all."

They were at the bike stand. Meredith lowered her head and kicked at the ground. "I don't *understand* you any more, Corrie," she said, raising her face. It was deeply flushed. "I thought we were *best friends*."

"We are!" said Corrie helplessly.

"Then why won't you *talk* to me? Why won't you tell me what's *wrong*? Is it something to do with your family? Could my *mum* help?"

Corrie considered this. Could she? She imagined pouring out her concerns about Sebastian to kind Mrs. Cooper. She might hug Corrie; that would be nice. But then she would tell Fa.

Corrie's chest ached. It would be such a relief to confide in Meredith. But she couldn't be sure she wouldn't tell her mother.

"There's nothing you can do," she muttered. "I just want to be left alone, all right?" Then she winced at how much she sounded like Sebastian.

"*Fine!*" Meredith said crossly. There were tears in her eyes. "I've tried and *tried* to help you, Corrie. I thought we were friends, but obviously we're *not!*"

She got on her bike and sped away. Corrie watched her, then picked up her own bike. She was so worn out she could hardly ride it home.

As she approached the shabby grey house she realized how little she wanted to go in the door. Home wasn't a refuge any more. She didn't have Sebastian. She didn't even have the Round Table. And now she'd lost Meredith as well.

THAT FRIDAY, ROZ was spending the night at Joyce's. Harry had gone to Victoria for the weekend with Peter's family. Fa was at a meeting until nine o'clock.

Sebastian didn't turn up for dinner.

"Where is he?" Corrie asked as Roz got ready to leave. "Was he at school?"

"I saw him at lunch. He must have gone to the library as usual."

"But he always comes home for dinner!"

"He's probably just late. Look, Corrie, I'm sure he'll be here soon. I have to go—Joyce's parents are taking us to see *The Ten Commandments*. Make sure the twins have a bath. They buried their dead turtles and they're filthy."

By eight o'clock Corrie was frantic. She had looked all around the back yard and peeked into Camelot, but no one was there. She gave the twins a hurried bath. "Where's Sebastian?" asked Orly.

"I don't know," said Corrie. When she saw how worried he and Juliet looked, she forced her voice to be calmer. "He's probably still at the library. He'll get home after you're asleep." She put them to bed without a story, ignoring their protests.

Then she sat at the bottom of the stairs. *A knight is brave. A knight never cries.*

What should she do? Phone someone ... First she tried the library, after a great deal of trouble finding the number in the book.

There was no answer. The library was closed.

Trying to stay calm, Corrie dialled Joyce's number. No answer there, either. They must still be at the movie.

If only Fa would get home! Corrie tried his number at the university, but she knew no one would answer—his meeting was downtown. She hung up the phone and paced around the house. Now it was eight-thirty. At least Fa would be here in half an hour. But what was Sebastian doing? Was he all right? Had he been in an accident, like Mum? If anyone found him, they wouldn't know who he was.

A knight is brave. A knight never cries ... Corrie sat on the stairs again, clenching her fist. She watched the hands on the grandfather clock inch their way to nine o'clock.

Then it was 9:10 and 9:20 and 9:40, and still Fa didn't appear. Now it was dark.

Was there anyone else she could phone? Meredith's parents. Corrie dialled the number with shaking fingers, but they weren't there. Aunt Madge ... she was far away in Winnipeg, but at least she could tell Corrie what to do.

Aunt Madge didn't answer either. Mrs. Oliphant? Corrie didn't know her number.

She went upstairs and checked on Orly and Juliet, envying their deep, unknowing sleep. She went into Sebastian's room and curled up like a pretzel on his bed. Everyone had abandoned her. There was no one to help.

A knight never cries. Corrie gazed at all the pictures of knights and their paraphernalia on the walls. What had happened to Sebastian?

Sir Lancelot would expect her to be Sir Gareth. Corrie sat up and tried to remember what to do when you needed help. This wasn't a fire, but surely it counted as an emergency.

She ran downstairs to the phone and tried to muster the courage to dial the operator. What would she say and what would the operator answer? Would she call the police? Would everyone think she was overreacting? Maybe Fa and Sebastian would come home after all.

It didn't matter what anyone thought. It was more important to find Sebastian.

Just as she lifted up the receiver the front door opened. Fa!

Corrie flew into his arms. "Oh, Fa!" she sobbed. "Sebastian has disappeared and I don't know what to do!" She began crying so hard she almost choked.

"My dear child!" Fa sat down in the hall chair and took her into his lap. "Whatever has upset you so much? Sebastian isn't here? Could he be at a friend's?"

"He hasn't g-got any friends! He didn't come home for dinner. And you didn't come home either and I was so scared!"

"Oh, my poor child ..." Fa held her closer. "I'm so sorry. The meeting went longer than I planned, but I've often been late before. And where are the others?"

"Roz is out and Harry's away! I'm all alone, except for the twins. And I've been so worried! Oh, Fa, there's something *wrong* with Sebastian!" Slowly, in between sobs, Corrie poured out all that had happened. She wept and wept on Fa's shoulder, limp with relief. Finally someone could help.

Fa looked astounded. "But why didn't you tell me this? My poor boy, I had no idea he was in this state!"

"Because you were working on your book! Because you don't like us to bother you! And Roz said he'd get better, but he didn't. And now he's disappeared!"

"My book ..." Fa shook his shaggy head as if he were waking up. "As if my book was more important than my son." Tears filled his eyes. "Oh, my dear Cordelia, I am so sorry you felt that way. I'm so very sorry."

Gently he wiped her wet face with his large handkerchief and let her blow her nose. Then he kissed her and set her on her feet. "Now, what are we going to do, eh? Do you have any idea where Sebastian could be? Could he be somewhere outside?"

Corrie thought hard. "I've looked in the shed and all around the yard. Maybe Joyous Gard ..."

"Joyous Gard?"

"That's what we called our fort on the golf course. It's Sir Lancelot's castle."

"We'll go there right away. I'll get a flashlight."

"But what about the twins? We can't leave them alone."

Fa seemed to come even more awake. "Of course we can't. What am I thinking? I know—we'll get Betty Tait from next door to come in for a while."

He phoned Mrs. Tait, who said she'd come right over. The neighbours ... Why hadn't Corrie thought of that? She could have phoned one of them for help, even though they had hardly spoken to the neighbours since Mum died.

In a few minutes Mrs. Tait was there. She stared at them curiously, but Fa didn't explain any more. He got a flashlight and told Corrie to put on her jacket.

"What if he's not there?" Corrie asked fearfully, as they walked down the sidewalk. The streetlights made pools of light on the pavement.

"Then we'll phone the police," said Fa. "Don't worry, my dear, we'll find him." He sounded as if he were trying to convince himself as well as Corrie.

The golf course at night was just as spooky as it had been at Hallowe'en. Dark trees loomed over them, and something large scuttled into the bushes as they went by—probably a raccoon, Fa said. His flashlight beamed a long tube of light that lit up the rough grass ahead of them. Corrie gripped Fa's dry hand tighter and he kept her from stumbling.

"There it is!" Corrie let go of Fa's hand and raced over the grass to the clearing. "Sebastian!" she called.

No one answered. Corrie led Fa into the bushes and held open the blanket they used as a door. Fa lit up the inside of Joyous Gard.

Sebastian was crouched in a corner of the fort, his arms around his knees. He was naked, except for a strip of cloth around his waist. His face and arms and legs were scratched and muddy. He shrank away from the beam of light and moaned like a trapped animal.

"Sebastian, my dear, dear boy ..." said Fa, going in. He handed the flashlight to Corrie. Sebastian stared as if he didn't know who they were. His eyes were wide and blank, like black holes in his white face.

"It's all right, my boy. We've come to take you home." Fa's voice was gentle and calm. He squatted in front of Sebastian, who kept staring at his father. Then his eyes focused and he gave a short, anguished cry.

Fa held out his arms. Sebastian unfolded into them. His thin bare shoulders shuddered with sobs. "I want *Mum* ..." he croaked. "I want her so much!"

Fa began to cry as well. "Oh, my sweet son," he whispered. He stroked Sebastian's hair. "So do I ... so do I."

THEY TOOK HIM HOME, Fa half carrying him.

"Oh, my goodness, what's happened?" cried Mrs. Tait as they pushed through the front door.

"It's all right, Betty," said Fa gruffly. "We can deal with this. Thank you so much for coming over."

"Can I help?"

Somehow Fa managed to get her to leave. Mrs. Tait had looked so concerned and kind, Corrie almost wished she could stay.

Fa led Sebastian to the bathroom, and Corrie listened to him tenderly bathing her brother as if he were a little boy. Then he gave him some aspirin, put him to bed, and sat beside him until he fell asleep. Corrie put on her pyjamas, then waited outside Sebastian's room on the hall rug, clutching her knees and leaning against the wall. Her body felt as if it were floating.

"He's fast asleep," whispered Fa, coming out of the room. "Come along, my dear child, you must go to bed as well." He picked up Corrie as if she were a baby and tucked her into bed. He kissed her, then stroked her head for a long time. Corrie sank into sleep as if into a soft nest where there were no troubles any more.

17

No More Pencils, No More Books

Sebastian had to go to the hospital for two weeks. He was weak from lack of proper nutrition, and he talked every day with a psychiatrist who worked with troubled teenagers.

Fa told them all this gravely. He went to see Sebastian every afternoon. The rest of the family wasn't allowed to.

They took refuge in one another. Juliet slept in Roz's room and Orly slept with Corrie. He curled into her like a comma, and his earthy little-boy smell soothed her. Harry had Hamlet to sleep with.

Fa ignored his book and sat with them in the den every night after dinner. He told them that Sebastian was doing as well as could be expected.

"He's eating more and getting lots of sleep. And he's crying a lot ... so am I," said Fa sheepishly. "Dr. Samuel says that's good for both of us."

"*I* cry all the time!" boasted Orly.

"That's because you're a crybaby," said Harry. "A knight *never* cries. That's what Sebastian always said."

"Did he?" Fa said. "I think he's wrong about that. Sometimes even knights have to cry."

Sebastian was due home the day after school finished. Corrie dreaded it. She couldn't get out of her head the image of his grimy face, his haunted eyes, and the deep sadness in those eyes.

On the Monday after they had found Sebastian, Corrie marched up to Meredith and blurted, "I'm sorry!" She had to get it out quickly.

"Oh, *Corrie*, I'm sorry too! Can we be best friends again?"

"Of course!" Corrie tried to tell Meredith about Sebastian.

Meredith looked puzzled. "Did he actually think he *was* Sir Lancelot?"

"I guess so," said Corrie. "I don't really understand it. The doctor told Fa he had 'lost his grasp of reality.' Fa says Sebastian flew too close to the sun."

"What does *that* mean?"

Corrie tried to explain about Icarus, but it was too complicated.

"Will Sebastian be *okay*?"

"I hope so. They say he needs a long rest."

Talking about Sebastian was embarrassing. With relief, they turned to the topic that was the rage in 6A—Sharon's approaching party.

Sharon was having their whole class to a party the evening of their graduation from Duke of Connaught. She was famous for her fancy parties, but Corrie had never been asked to one before.

"It's a *mixed* party," said Meredith nervously. "I've never been to one, have you?"

Corrie shuddered. "No! Do we have to go?"

"*I* want to, but I won't unless you do."

Corrie had no choice. "Okay, I'll go," she sighed.

Meredith looked determined. "I think it will be *fun*. What should we *wear*, though? We have to get dressed up for the ceremony in the afternoon. Do you think my chemise is too plain? I *could* wear my yellow organdy, but it might be too small. Sharon said we should wear something more casual for the party."

Corrie listened to this chatter with horror, deeply regretting that she had agreed to go.

The next day, the hottest day of the year, the new Second Narrows Bridge collapsed, killing nineteen people. All week Fa and the Coopers and Mr. Zelmach talked about the disaster, but their grave voices floated high above Corrie's head. She tried to feel sorry for the victims' families, but it was the same as when the grown-ups discussed the H-bomb or the Russian menace—it seemed to have nothing to do with her own world. Her head was full enough worrying about Sebastian—and about the party.

Then Roz took her in hand. She asked Fa for some extra money, and she and Corrie went to Oakridge. First Corrie got her bangs trimmed. Then Roz selected some red pedal-pushers and a matching polka-dot sleeveless blouse for her. The cuffs on the pants matched the pattern on the blouse, and they even found red runners.

"That's perfect for the party," said Roz. "Now, what about the ceremony? I got really dressed up for mine. I wish you could wear my dress, but you're taller than I am now—it would be too short."

"I am?" said Corrie in amazement. Roz had them stand back to back in the dressing-room mirror. It was true! Her head was about half an inch taller than Roz's. No wonder her legs had felt so long in the last few months!

"Fa said to spend as much as we liked. Let's find you something really nice."

Before Corrie could protest, Roz had picked out a cornflower blue organdy dress and a stiff crinoline. Then she bought her black shoes with straps that swung back behind the heels to turn them into pumps, and new white socks. Corrie stared shyly at the stranger in the mirror.

"You're getting to be as pretty as Mum," said Roz softly.

GRADUATION WAS MUCH MORE fun than Corrie expected. School ended at noon. As soon as the bell rang the class shouted,

No more pencils,
No more books!
No more teachers'
Dirty looks!

Mr. Zelmach made a terrible face as they rushed past him out the door.

After lunch Corrie washed her face and hands and changed into her new dress.

"You look like a princess!" said Orly when she came down the stairs.

"You look very nice, Cordelia," Fa told her. Corrie held his hand as they walked back to school together. Her stiff dress kept bumping into his side.

Corrie waved to Fa from the stage, proud of how distinguished he looked in the crowd of parents. After the ceremony, as she stood beside him clutching her certificate, Mr. Zelmach came up and shook Fa's hand.

"I'm very pleased to meet you, Professor Bell," he said. "Corrie has been a credit to the class, and she's sure to do well in junior high—even in arithmetic, right, Corrie? I'll see you at the concert!" He walked away to greet more parents.

"What concert?" said Fa, looking befuddled as usual.

Corrie grinned. "I told you about it a long time ago, Fa! In July we're singing in a concert to celebrate B.C.'s centennial. We have to go downtown with a lot of other schools."

"Remind me of the date and I'll be sure to come," said Fa.

"You will?"

"Of course I will! And I'm sorry I haven't met your teacher before now. He seems like a nice young man."

Young? Mr. Zelmach had told them he was thirty-six! But Corrie supposed he must seem young to Fa.

After school Corrie tore off her dress and prickly crinoline and got into the red pedal-pushers and top. Meredith's father drove them to the party. Sharon's house was as large as the Bells', but it was clean and tidy and smelled like beeswax. Corrie's heart thudded as they entered the rumpus room. It seemed like a room full of strangers. The girls giggled and whispered on one side and the boys stood silently on the other, eyeing the food.

Corrie wanted to bolt. But slowly the party improved. Sharon's mother pinned papers on every person's back with half of the name of a nursery rhyme on them, like "Jack," "Fiddle," or "Humpty." They had to go around and find the rest of their rhyme by asking questions. The questions and laughter made everyone relax and remember that they were still the same people as every day in school.

Then Sharon's aunt arrived to teach them square dancing. Corrie enjoyed prancing around as the woman called out, "Swing your pardner, do-si-do!" No one had to worry about being asked to dance; they picked numbers and chose partners that way.

Corrie's was Jamie. The two of them giggled as they stepped on each other's toes. They sat together as they ate the delicious sundaes Sharon's mother had made.

On the way home in the car Meredith whispered, "You're so lucky you got Jamie instead of awful Frank, the way I did! Do you *like* him?"

Corrie squirmed. "Sure, I like him. He's much nicer than he used to be. But he's just a boy in our class, nothing special," she added firmly. It was important to nip any silliness of Meredith's in the bud.

To "nip in the bud ..." Aunt Madge used to say that. Corrie wondered if Fa had told Aunt Madge about Sebastian. The lightness of the day left her, and she began to worry about tomorrow.

18

The Death of Sir Lancelot

Corrie woke up on June 27 with her usual airy first-day-of-the-summer-holidays feeling. Then she remembered: Sebastian was coming home that afternoon.

She spent the morning at Meredith's, helping her pack. The Coopers were taking the train that evening to Alberta, to stay at Mrs. Cooper's parents' cottage for all of July. "I *wish* you could come too, Corrie," Meredith told her.

"Never mind," her mother said. "We'll be back in August, and you two can have a joint birthday party. Won't that be fun?"

Corrie smiled. She would miss Mrs. Cooper almost as much as she would miss Meredith. She stayed for lunch, and then she couldn't prolong going home any longer. At least the Coopers' hugs gave her strength.

"Let's grow our hair this summer!" said Meredith. "Then this fall we can have *ponytails!*"

"Okay," grinned Corrie.

"Please give our regards to your family, Corrie," said Mrs. Cooper. "I'm sure you'll find that your brother is much better."

All the way home Corrie prayed that this would be true.

Fa went off in a taxi to get Sebastian. Roz, Corrie, Harry, Juliet, and Orly all waited in the living room. Even the twins had nothing to say.

"He's here!" Juliet rushed to the door, Orly close behind her.

Sebastian walked in as casually as if he were coming home from school on an ordinary day. "Hello, everybody," he said quietly.

Corrie gasped. He had cut his hair! His beautiful knightly hair was as short as any other teenaged boy's, slicked back from his forehead with cream. He had gained weight and his skin had cleared up, but his grey eyes were dull.

Roz brought in a jug of lemonade.

"Are you still sick, Sebastian?" Juliet asked.

"Juliet! That's rude!" said Roz.

"It's all right," said Sebastian. "No, Juliet, I'm not still sick. I'm much better. And I'm sorry I caused you all so much trouble."

Corrie shivered. His voice was careful and even, as if he had rehearsed his words.

"Trouble!" Fa put his hand on Sebastian's shoulder. "This was my fault, my boy, not yours. Listen, my dears, I have many things I want to tell you."

Fa actually looked frightened of them. They put down their glasses and gave him their full attention.

Fa apologized for neglecting them since Mum had died. He said that he should have noticed far sooner that Sebastian was unhappy. "I've been escaping these past years into my work," he said. "I suppose it was my way of grieving for your mother. Just as Sebastian escaped into being Sir Lancelot, right, my boy? But that's all over now. Sebastian and I have been doing a lot of talking. We're both going to try to live more in reality, right?"

Sebastian nodded stiffly as Fa continued. "It's unfair that Sebastian and Rosalind and Cordelia had to take care of everything. *I* should have been doing that, not assuming Mrs. Oliphant was."

"We hate her!" said Juliet.

Fa smiled. "I know you found her difficult. Well, she found you difficult too! Several times I had to raise her salary to keep her from leaving. A month ago, however, she gave me her notice. I persuaded her to stay until school was out. Yesterday was her last day with us."

"Yay!" shouted Orly.

Corrie hadn't even noticed that the Elephant wasn't here today. And Mrs. Oliphant hadn't said goodbye to them. She probably disliked them as much as they disliked her. None of them had ever asked her anything personal. They had ignored her, as if she were a robot, because that was how Sebastian wanted it.

"But who will do all the cooking and cleaning?" asked Roz. "We can manage in the summer, but what about after we're back at school?"

"Don't worry, Rosalind. In the fall we'll find someone you like. I'll make sure of that. And this summer *I'm* going to take care of the house."

They gaped at him. "You?"

"Don't look so surprised! I used to cook quite a lot before I met your mother—I was a confirmed old bachelor when she married me, remember. And anyone can clean. I want to spend more time with you, and I want to give you a rest. It's not right that children your age should have to do all that you've been doing."

"But what about your book?" asked Corrie.

"I've told my publishers that my book has been indefinitely postponed." Fa gazed at them fondly. "If there's one thing I've learned from all this, it's that you are infinitely more important than any book."

Bubbles of hope rose in Corrie. Fa loved them! He was going to take care of them!

But Sebastian's new appearance and empty eyes and bland voice scared her. Still, at least he was home, and he looked much healthier. Surely he would soon become his old self again. Surely everything was going to be fine.

FOR A MONTH it almost was. Every morning Fa got up early and cooked them pancakes or bacon and eggs. He vacuumed and polished and dusted and wouldn't let anyone help. "Go and play!" he ordered. He hired people to get rid of the mice and the silverfish, to repair the sagging gate, to cut the vine in Corrie's room, and to prune and weed the garden.

The house shone as it hadn't for years; Corrie thought it seemed grateful for all the attention, the way it had at Christmas. The air smelled of baking or casseroles, just as it had when Aunt Madge lived with them.

Corrie woke up in her clean room every morning feeling almost carefree. Her only worry was the person she always worried about—Sebastian.

The day before Sebastian had come home, Fa had told them, "Sebastian will be all right eventually, but he'll be going through many changes. It's as if he has shed one self and is growing a new one. You'll have to be patient while he finds out who that self is."

Corrie found it hard to be patient. Sebastian was like a polite stranger who was visiting the family. He had neglected his schoolwork so much last term that he was taking two courses over again at summer school so he could enter high school in the fall. He spent a lot of time studying. When he wasn't, he taught the twins how to ride the new bikes Fa had bought them, or he went to the swimming pool or the library with Corrie and Harry. He joined the family on expeditions to the beach or to Stanley Park. Even he and Roz were friends again. He teased her about Ronnie and she helped him with math, which she was good at.

The trouble was, Sebastian was *too* polite and helpful. His smile was artificial and his words continued to sound rehearsed. He only spoke when spoken to and the rest of the time was eerily silent. It was as if he were pretending to be normal the way he used to pretend to be Sir Lancelot.

Worst of all, he didn't confide in Corrie. Fa talked to him a lot; almost every evening he visited Sebastian in his room. Corrie felt jealous every time she saw the closed door.

One evening she tried knocking on it after Fa had gone downstairs. "Hi, Corrie," said Sebastian, with the strained smile that made Corrie wince. "Did you want something?"

Corrie shrugged. "I just wanted to say hi. How are you?" she asked softly.

"I'm fine," said Sebastian.

"Did you ... did you have a nice time at the doctor's today?" Once a week Sebastian visited Dr. Samuel. Fa talked to the psychiatrist on another day. He said he was learning how to be a father again.

"It was all right."

"What do you talk about?" asked Corrie.

"Oh, lots of things." Corrie knew from his closed expression that he wouldn't tell her more.

"Do you like him?"

Sebastian flushed. "He's okay. Corrie, it's very nice to talk to you, but I have a lot of homework to do."

Corrie skittered out, mortified at her dumb questions. How different this was from the easy conversations between Lancelot and Gareth!

Juliet kept asking Sebastian when they were going to have a Round Table meeting. "We haven't had one for a long time, and me and Orly want to be squires!" she complained.

"You can play at knights all you want," Sebastian told her. "But I'm too old for that now."

Corrie tried to take his place again by assembling the remaining members of the Round Table. Harry was pleased to be dubbed Sir Tristan—his trial was to eat a worm, which he did easily. Juliet and Orly were promoted to squires. The knights and squires had rousing tilting contests and sword fights in the yard, but Corrie couldn't bear to go to Joyous Gard after that awful night.

The next day, after roll call, as Sir Gareth was reading them a story, he put down the book.

"It's no use," said Corrie, getting to her feet.

"What's the matter?" asked Harry.

"I can't play this game any more. I guess ... I guess I'm just too old for it. You can be the head knight, Harry. You can all be knights. You can even choose your own names."

"You mean I can be *Sir Lancelot*?" asked Harry.

"No!" said Corrie. Tears stung her eyes. "Anyone but him. Sir Lancelot is dead!"

Before they could respond, she ran out of the shed and up to her room. Sir Gareth was dead, too. In a way, Sir Lancelot had killed him, just like in the legend.

I'll never be a knight again, Corrie thought. She tried to cry some more, but after a few minutes it didn't seem important enough to cry about. She picked up her novel and became immersed in the adventures of the Borrowers. At least books were still magic.

For the next few days the house and yard were full of knights furiously knocking swords or lances together. Then the game petered out—the three remaining knights couldn't think of anything else to do but fight each other.

Corrie spent a whole day tidying up the shed. She threw away broken weapons and swept the floor. She gathered up pennants and armour and schedules and hawking hoods, put them in a box, wrote "Round Table stuff" on it, and pushed it into a corner. For a second she gazed sadly at it, but she had to get to her swimming class, and she ran out of the shed.

FA WAS MUCH MORE attuned to them now. He noticed that Juliet had lost a tooth and talked to Harry about being nicer to Orly. They sucked up his attention like thirsty sponges. Juliet stopped biting her nails, and Orly stopped being afraid of the dark. Roz teased Fa about his chubby middle and made him buy a new cardigan to replace the holey one he always wore. Best of all, Corrie often crawled into Fa's lap, even though she was getting so tall that she almost fell off.

Fa started talking about Mum. Every evening he encouraged them to remember her.

Roz could recall the most. "Mum took yoga classes," she said. "Every day she'd get into her tights and do strange poses on the living-room rug. I used to try to copy her"—she giggled—"but I always fell over."

"Did she sing a song about three little people in a boat?" asked Harry slowly.

Fa sang softly. "'Wynken, Blynken, and Nod, one night / Sailed off in a wooden shoe ...'"

Harry grinned.

Corrie remembered how she had helped Mum try new, exotic recipes, like chili con carne or Swiss fondue.

"They tasted awful!" laughed Fa. "But that didn't deter her."

Mum smelled like ginger, thought Corrie, and laughed merrily, and talked loudly like Juliet.

"*I* remember she rubbed my back every night before I went to sleep," said Orly.

"I can't remember *anything*," Juliet said. "And I don't think you do either, Orly. You're just making it up."

"I am not!"

"Perhaps he isn't, even though he was only three," said Fa. "Molly did rub his back every night—it was the only way to get him to sleep. Would you like me to start rubbing your back again, Orlando?"

"Yes, please," whispered Orly.

Sebastian never contributed to any of these conversations. But Corrie watched him closely, and sometimes his eyes would light up briefly, as if a flame were being ignited.

It was sad to talk about Mum, like watching a shimmering, fragile bubble float in the air and then burst. But it was also comforting. The more they remembered, the more memories there seemed to be.

ONE MORNING Fa took them up to Mum's studio, the room on the third floor that was always closed. He pulled up the blinds and showed them all of her paintings. Corrie gazed in wonder at the bright canvases. They were like lights beaming from the wall. She had forgotten that Mum had done all of these.

Juliet danced around the studio as if the paintings were an audience. Sebastian seemed mesmerized, staring intently at each one.

"These are amazing," he whispered. For the first time since he'd come home his voice sounded like his own.

"This picture is laughing!" said Orly, standing in front of a canvas streaked with yellow and blue.

"You're absolutely right, Orlando. It *is* laughing," said Fa. He told them how Mum had hoped to have a show. "There was a gallery downtown that was really interested in her. She was trying to get a few more paintings done to have enough."

"Couldn't you get in touch with the gallery?" asked Roz. "It might still be interested!"

"I could ..." said Fa slowly. "But it means that people might buy them, and they're so good, I think they would sell easily. Then we'd never see them again."

"But we never did *really* see these," said Corrie. "We only saw the ones in the living room."

Fa smiled at her. "You're right, Cordelia. Perhaps it's better that Molly's paintings be out in the world rather than hidden in a room. She would certainly have preferred that. I just don't know if I'm ready to part with them yet. Of course, we could keep our favourites. The trouble is, they're *all* my favourites! I'll think about it ..."

That night Corrie dreamt about Mum. Corrie was flying from a trapeze and Mum was watching her, laughing and clapping. Corrie told Roz about it.

"Oh, Corrie, you're so lucky!" said Roz. "I try and try to dream about Mum. Every night I think of her before I go to sleep, but she never comes!"

"You can pretend my dream was yours, if you like," offered Corrie.

THE CENTENNIAL CONCERT was on July 13. Corrie was surprised at how glad she was to see her class again. She'd been so immersed in the family she'd forgotten about them. Darlene greeted her eagerly, and Jamie came right up and told her about his camping trip. Several people were away for the summer, like Meredith. Corrie suddenly missed her. But in two more weeks she'd be home!

They stood on risers on a stage and sang their three songs with hundreds of other voices in the hot sun. Corrie had been afraid she'd forget the words, but they had rehearsed them so often that it was easy. Mr. Zelmach couldn't stop telling them how proud he was of them. Everyone in the family except Sebastian, who was still at summer school, came to hear Corrie. They told her they were proud, too.

ONE DAY FA WENT OUT in the afternoon and said he'd be home in time to make dinner. They were all sitting on the back steps, licking Jell-O powder out of their palms, when they heard a car on the street honking again and again.

"Go and see who that is," Corrie told Harry. "They must have the wrong house."

Harry ran to the front of the house. Then they heard him shout, "Corrie, Roz, everyone! Come out here right now!"

They found Fa standing in front of a gleaming red-and-white station wagon, grinning like a little boy. "Come and meet your new car!" he said.

"A *car*, a *car*!" With shrieks and questions they surrounded the car, stroking its shiny surface. Then they clambered inside. Even with the twins stretched out in the back there was plenty of room.

"I thought you didn't know how to drive!" said Harry.

"Of course I do!" said Fa. "I just haven't for a few years. I stopped after ... I stopped after your mother's accident. I didn't think I ever wanted to drive again, but now I do. It's too inconvenient for all of you, not having someone to drive you places. Do you like it? It's a Buick. It's only two years old—I bought it from a colleague. The colour is rather bright, but it runs well."

"I *adore* it," said Roz, stroking the red-and-white leather seats.

"Look at the neat steering wheel," said Harry, turning it back and forth. "It looks like a flying saucer!"

"We could *sleep* back here!" called Juliet from the back.

Corrie snuggled into the comfortable seats. They had a car, like other families!

"Let's go and pick up Sebastian at school!" said Fa. They slammed the doors shut, and the sleek car glided along the street like a purring tiger. The twins kept opening the windows and sticking their heads out, until Fa told them to stop.

"Sebastian, Sebastian, we have a car!" yelled Juliet as soon as they spotted him.

Sebastian walked up to them. "A car ... It's very nice." His voice was as even as usual.

"In a year I'll teach you how to drive it," Fa told him.

"And in two years I can drive too!" Roz threw her arms around her father. "Oh, Fa, this summer is perfect!"

How could she say that? thought Corrie. The car was swell, and having Fa so involved with the family again seemed like a miracle. But her brother sat woodenly in the back seat, staring out the window with no expression.

Sir Lancelot was dead, but where was Sebastian?

19

Sebastian

Corrie got a postcard from Meredith. It said she was staying in Alberta for the rest of the summer, to go to a camp with her cousin. "They have riding and canoeing and we'll live in tents. It will be so much fun! Mum and Dad are staying longer at the lake. I'll bring your birthday present home with me! Sorry I won't see you until the fall. Love, Meredith."

Corrie blinked back her tears. Meredith didn't seem very sorry—she seemed to have almost forgotten Corrie. Corrie had been planning to decorate their bikes for the contest at the community centre, and to go swimming at the pool every day. And what about their joint birthday party? Now August seemed like a blank.

Corrie felt a bit better when Fa told them he was taking them on a holiday to celebrate Sebastian's finishing summer school. They asked the Taits to look in on Hamlet and Jingle every day. They filled the back of the station wagon with suitcases, towels, and beach toys, took the ferry to Vancouver Island, and drove up island to a place called Oyster River.

The drive took hours. The twins sang "Purple People Eater" until the others begged them to stop. They played I Packed My Grandmother's Trunk and I Spy.

They stayed in a motel right on the beach. Every day they braved the cold waves and ran around on the firm sand. Corrie helped the younger ones construct a driftwood fort. They floated down the river in the motel's wooden kayaks and played on the swing set outside the cabins. Every night Fa cooked them hamburgers or hot dogs in their little kitchen.

Harry, Juliet, and Orly soon made friends with the many other children staying in the motel. They all roamed around in a gang, carrying sticks and slingshots, their feet caked with sand and their noses sunburnt. Fa called them the Reign of Terror. Roz was thrilled to find someone from her school; every day she and Paula sat on the beach, reading movie magazines and improving their tans.

Corrie joined the gang of kids every evening to play red rover but, apart from that, she kept to herself. She knew she should make an effort to make friends with three girls who were her age, but they seemed such a tight group that she was too shy to attempt it.

Instead she hung around with Fa. He still seemed like a precious new friend. They walked to the river, or to the store to buy food, or they read their books together. Fa taught her the names of birds and shells, and how to play chess.

Sebastian either sat in a chair on the porch, hidden behind his own book, or walked for miles on the beach. He was more silent than ever, and Corrie had given up trying to communicate with him.

On their last evening Fa took them to a restaurant in Courtney to celebrate Roz's and Harry's birthdays, which were a day apart. When they got back, Fa and Corrie went for one more walk on the beach. The waves broke on the sand like a sigh, as if they knew the family was leaving.

Corrie took Fa's hand. "Is Sebastian ever going to be all right?" she asked.

Fa sighed. "The poor boy ... He's just not sure how to relate to the world now. But Dr. Samuel says he's doing well. Don't worry, Cordelia, he'll soon be more like his old self. Not the sick old self, but the best one."

Corrie's voice broke. "But he seems so ... so flat! And he never talks to me!"

Fa put his arm around her. "He will. We can't hurry him, you know. Just give him time."

WHEN THEY GOT BACK to the city, Fa lost his enthusiasm for cooking. He slept later and they returned to their old habits of finding cereal for themselves. He took them out for dinners more often than he cooked.

Roz took over the cooking. Corrie helped her, and Harry became surprisingly enthusiastic, attacking a recipe in the same methodical way he did the instructions for a model.

Fa stopped cleaning too. He began spending time in his study. "I'm afraid that my book will die if I don't do at least a little work on it," he apologized.

"Can books die?" asked Juliet.

"They can lose their life if they're neglected. But don't worry, I'll work only a few hours a day. And feel free to disturb me any time you wish."

Very quickly, the hours lengthened. Soon Fa was in his study all day again. They went in and out of it in a way they never would have before, but no one liked to disturb him for long. When Fa emerged, however, he was much more focused on them than in the Round Table days, and he was still with them in the evenings.

The house became dusty and untidy once more. Sebastian still hid in his room, even though his classes were over. What was he doing in there? Corrie wondered.

Roz and Corrie made up schedules for the rest of August: one for cooking, one for cleaning and laundry, and one for looking after the twins.

Who was going to look after the household in the fall? wondered Corrie. She and Roz consulted with Fa, who said he had put in a request to an agency but hadn't heard back from them yet.

Corrie sighed. Another Mrs. Oliphant disturbing their peace. Fa had promised that the new person would be nicer than the Elephant, but she'd still be a stranger.

Corrie knocked on Fa's door one afternoon. "Fa, at Christmas Aunt Madge told me that Cousin Daphne was getting better. Do you know if she is? Do you think Aunt Madge could come back?" If only she could!

"Daphne *is* better," said Fa. "Last week I asked Madge if she could live with us again and she said she would really like to. But ..." He pressed his thumbs to his eyes, the way he did when he was worried. "Sebastian doesn't want her to come, Cordelia. I thought I'd better consult with him and he was quite adamant about it."

"But *why?*"

"He wouldn't tell me why, and I didn't like to press him."

"*I'll* ask him why!" How could Sebastian quash such a perfect solution?

"My dear, I really don't think that's a good idea. We don't want to upset Sebastian in any way. He's still very fragile, you know. If he doesn't want Madge to come, we can't have her. Don't say anything to the others about this. I'm sure the agency will find us someone good, don't you worry."

Sometimes Fa was still as authoritative as King Arthur. Corrie knew she had lost.

Roz found her in the den, morosely watching *Perry Mason*. "Corrie, I've just had a wonderful idea!"

"What?"

"Let's ask Fa if Aunt Madge can come back!"

"She can't. She has to look after Cousin Daphne," Corrie muttered.

"Couldn't we at least ask her? At Christmas she told me that Cousin Daphne was feeling better."

"Fa did ask her," said Corrie. "Cousin Daphne is worse again. Aunt Madge said she'd ... she'd really like to come, but she can't."

A knight never lies. But she was no longer a knight.

"Shoot!" Roz plunked herself down on the chesterfield. "I sure don't want to go through another housekeeper!"

Corrie got up and left before she had to lie any more.

AUGUST WAS BORING without Meredith back in the city. One rainy morning Corrie wandered through the house wondering what to do. She decided to start another diorama.

She got a glass of water, set up her paints on her desk, and began coating the back of a shoebox a rosy blue. When the paint had dried she added a line of low green hills and a rising sun.

Rooting around in the box of diorama materials she kept under her bed, Corrie found a piece of green velvet cloth. Aunt Madge had given her this once; it was left over from a cushion cover.

Corrie cut the cloth to fit the bottom of the box, then glued it in place. She smoothed the soft velvet—it looked just like grass.

An hour later the velvet had become a meadow. A tree made out of a branch covered with green paper leaves was anchored in place with Plasticine. A robin perched on one of its branches. Red and yellow felt flowers dotted the meadow, and a stream of blue ribbon meandered through it.

Corrie was pleased with the results, but the scene needed more. If only she could draw people! Then she could add a tiny figure of each member of the family. They could be having a picnic under the tree.

She couldn't draw people, but she'd always been excellent at drawing horses. She sketched six small horses on a piece of cardboard, coloured each one with pencil crayons and carefully cut them out with nail scissors. It took forever to carve out each tiny leg and ear and tail.

She glued tabs on the backs of the horses and arranged them in the meadow. Fa was a golden palomino standing under the shade of the tree. Twin grey ponies munched the flowers. A chestnut (Corrie), an Appaloosa (Roz), and a pinto (Harry) stood nose to nose in the middle. On the right side of the meadow—but facing the others—was a handsome black stallion.

Corrie stared at the scene and then she made one more horse— a white one with a flowing mane. She placed it under the tree beside Fa.

It was finished. Corrie wished herself into the scene, relishing the smell of the sweet grass, the sound of the bubbling stream and the bird's song welcoming the dawn. She had created a little paradise. Mum was with them again and everyone was at peace. No one had to worry about a new school or a new housekeeper or whether Sebastian would ever be better. If Corrie were really a horse in a meadow she would roll over on the grass and kick up her heels for joy.

But she wasn't. She gazed at the diorama and sighed. At least she could look at it sometimes.

CORRIE STARTED GOING to the pool every afternoon, after her stint of twinsitting was over. She was teaching herself how to do a better dive. She had always found it hard not to splash or to flip her legs over. She crouched at the side of the pool and dived again and again. On the third day she thought she'd improved enough to try the board.

"Good try!" someone cried. "Curl your toes under and spring out more. Do you want me to show you?"

Darlene! Corrie was about to shake her head and walk away. Why would Darlene want to have anything to do with her? But she seemed so friendly. "I guess you could," said Corrie shyly. "Do you know how to dive?"

Darlene walked to the board, bounced on the end, and executed a perfect dive.

"Wow!" said Corrie after Darlene had climbed out of the pool. "Where did you learn that?"

"My dad taught me," said Darlene. "I can show you. Come on."

For an hour Darlene showed Corrie how to bounce high and keep her legs taut. By the end of the afternoon Corrie almost had it.

"Do you want to try again tomorrow?" asked Darlene.

"Sure!" Corrie wondered why Darlene was at the pool by herself when she was usually with the rest of the Five. "Where are the others?" she asked casually as they changed.

"Everyone's away," said Darlene glumly. "They're at their summer cabins or visiting relatives. Where's Meredith?"

"She's in Alberta for the whole summer. She was supposed to come back for August, but then she decided to go to some stupid camp."

"A camp—yuck, I'd hate that. Everyone telling you what to do all the time. Do you want a Popsicle?"

"I haven't got any money."

"I'll treat you. Come on." They walked to the concession booth, Darlene chattering all the way. Corrie licked her orange Popsicle with awe. Darlene had always been nice to her, but now she was asking her to come to her house on the way home!

"I'll show you the new clothes my mum bought me for school," she told Corrie.

For the last two weeks of the summer Corrie saw Darlene every day. They swam or went bowling or rode their bikes to Little Mountain or played Monopoly with her little brothers. It wasn't as special as going to the Coopers'. Darlene's brothers whined, and her mother was cranky.

A few times Corrie asked Darlene home. "I remember this old house!" said Darlene. "Isn't there a secret closet on the top floor?" Corrie had almost forgotten that before Mum died, Darlene had been her friend and had sometimes come over to play.

The two of them talked a lot about what junior high would be like. In a couple of weeks they would be going there! They shared their fears of the huge number of students and the enormous building, of having a lot of teachers and homework every night—and dances and older boys. "I like boys, but I'm not ready to date yet," Darlene confided. "Mum says I can't until grade nine."

"Date!" Corrie was horrified. She was *never* planning to date, but she didn't tell Darlene that. If she did, Darlene might think she was babyish.

Darlene was not like Meredith. She didn't read much and she didn't have Meredith's contagious enthusiasm. Her greatest interest was sports; she had won awards for skating as well as for swimming. She and Corrie spent hours throwing balls into her family's basketball hoop.

At least she was someone to hang around with until Meredith came back. And Corrie felt comforted sharing her own worries about Laburnum with Darlene. Darlene even asked if she and Meredith would like to walk to school with the Five on their first day. "I'll ask her," said Corrie, amazed.

Roz took Corrie shopping for new school clothes, and Darlene tagged along. Corrie refused to get the twin-set they suggested, but she was happy with her red car coat, her white blouses, and her kilt in the B.C. Centennial plaid.

"Do you want nylons?" asked Roz.

"*I* have nylons," said Darlene. "Grade seven is when you start wearing them, right, Roz?"

"We wear socks to school, but nylons for parties and church," Roz explained.

"No thanks," said Corrie. Part of her was intrigued by the idea of nylons, but she would wait and see what Meredith decided.

CORRIE'S BIRTHDAY WAS BETTER than she had expected. All of her presents were good ones, especially the Brownie camera Fa gave her. And Sebastian's smile seemed genuine when he handed her the last Narnia novel, the only one she hadn't read.

"How did you *know* I wanted that?" she asked.

"I heard you tell Roz," he mumbled.

Corrie chose the White Spot for her birthday dinner, and Darlene came, too. Darlene, however, spent the whole time talking to Roz about junior high. As Corrie sat in the restaurant relishing her fried chicken, she wondered what Meredith was doing. She could hear her voice saying, "We're both *twelve*!"

Corrie picked up her chicken and munched it as messily as the twins. If there was only one more year before she had to be a teenager, she might as well enjoy it.

THE AGENCY PHONED Fa with three names. He asked each woman over one at a time, letting the whole family interview her.

The first woman was called Miss White. She was as pale and bland as her name.

"What kind of games do you like to play?" asked Juliet, after the usual questions about cooking and housework.

"Games? Well, I like cards and checkers," said Miss White timidly.

"I don't mean *those* kind of games," said Juliet scornfully. "I mean things like cowboys and war and pirates."

"Those aren't nice things for little girls to play," said Miss White a little more firmly. "How about dolls? I could help you dress them."

"I hate dolls! Do you know what I did with my Betsey Wetsey? I cut off her head and—"

"That's enough, Juliet," said Fa. "We'll let you know, Miss White." He ushered her hastily out the door.

The second woman was quite nice, but Orly asked why she smelled funny and she left in a huff.

The third one was called Mrs. Morrissey. She was strong-looking and quiet. Mrs. Morrissey bravely told the twins she would help them trap a squirrel. She listened patiently while Harry told her about his rocket.

"This is a very large house to clean," said Fa. "Do you think you could manage it as well as the cooking, and help with looking after the twins?"

Mrs. Morrissey looked around the cluttered, dirty living room with longing, as if she could hardly wait to get at it. "I'm very good at cleaning," she told them. "I could manage it easily."

"I liked her," said Roz after she'd left. "She said she could teach me how to sew."

"She sounds like a good cook," said Harry.

The twins said they liked her too.

"What about you, Corrie?" asked Fa. "You didn't ask Mrs. Morrissey anything. Do you think we should hire her? She had an excellent recommendation from her last family."

Corrie shrugged. "She's fine." She tried to smile. "And she seems like the nicest one we've had so far."

"Sebastian? What do you think?" Sebastian had been as silent in the interviews as Corrie.

"I think she'll do very well," he said, sounding like someone in a book.

Fa looked relieved. "I'll offer her the position, then, and tell her she can start next week."

CORRIE TOOK AN APPLE from the kitchen and climbed Sentry. She had meant what she said. Mrs. Morrissey was nice. Everyone else seemed to really like her. But she was still just a housekeeper, not part of the family. She wouldn't be there in the evenings; she wouldn't sit with them at dinner or watch TV with them in the den. She wasn't Aunt Madge.

Corrie pitched her apple core to the ground. She gazed at Sebastian's window and saw the back of his head bent over something. All of this was his fault.

"We don't want to upset Sebastian in any way." She could hear Fa's words but she didn't care. She almost fell out of the tree, she climbed down so fast. She ran up the two flights of stairs and burst into Sebastian's room, panting and hot.

Sebastian spun around from his desk. "Corrie! What's wrong?"

"Everything is wrong!" said Corrie. "Especially *you*!"

She marched up to him and shook him. "Why did you tell Fa that Aunt Madge can't come back? Don't you see how much we need her? She *wants* to come! You're the only person who's stopping her!"

Her words shot out like arrows from Robin Hood's bow. She couldn't stop them. "Why don't you *talk* to me any more? Why do you hide away from us all? What's the matter with you, Sebastian? Why have you changed so much?"

Corrie was breathing so heavily she had to sit down on the bed. Her cheeks burned and she hid her face in her hands to cool them.

Sebastian sat down beside her. "Corrie ..." She looked up at him. "Corrie, listen. I'll try to explain."

As he talked, her heart lifted. Sebastian sounded like Sebastian. His voice was so low she had to strain to hear, but it was his old voice, impassioned and strong.

"When Fa asked me if I wanted Aunt Madge to come back I just couldn't let her. I was so awful to her! I was unfriendly and mean, two years ago and at Christmas. I ... I don't like to think of myself like that. It's not how—"

"It's not how a knight behaves," whispered Corrie.

He nodded sadly. "Right. It's not how a knight behaves or how *anyone* should behave. If Aunt Madge was here I'd feel ashamed every time I looked at her. And she would be embarrassed. She's a good person. I just never saw that because ... because she was taking Mum's place. She tried so hard to be like a mother to us. The rest of you liked that, but I couldn't stand it!"

Corrie had been keeping herself very still, afraid he might stop. Now, though, she had to interrupt. "But, Sebastian, why can't you just apologize? Aunt Madge would forgive you, I know. She knows you weren't yourself because of Mum's death. All you have to do is say you're sorry, and then she'd come!"

"You're absolutely right, Corrie. But I just can't bring myself to say it. Then I'd be admitting that I wasn't—"

"That you weren't perfect," said Corrie. A perfect gentle knight. "*No* one is perfect!" she told him.

"That's what Dr. Samuel keeps reminding me," said Sebastian ruefully.

Corrie had one more arrow to release. "Sebastian, aren't you thinking more about yourself than you are about us?"

The arrow hit its mark. Sebastian flushed and lowered his head. Corrie almost held her breath, afraid to say more.

She looked around the room. All the drawings of knights and castles were gone. In their place were other pictures, of birds. Beautiful drawings and watercolours. Eagles and wrens and herons and owls, all portrayed in meticulous detail.

Could Sebastian have done these? They were much better than the birds of prey he had drawn earlier; they were as good as pictures in a book.

Sebastian stood up. "Wait here. I'll be right back."

Corrie walked around the room and looked at the pictures again. They *were* Sebastian's! A few unfinished ones were on his desk, surrounded by bird books and pencils and paints. So this was what he'd been doing in here for the last few weeks!

Corrie curled up on the bed and closed her eyes. She almost fell asleep. It seemed hours until the door opened again.

"Wake up!" said her brother. He stood in the doorway. "I did it."

Corrie sat up groggily. "Did what?"

"I phoned her. I phoned Aunt Madge and asked her to come back. I told her I was sorry for being so nasty to her. She cried so much she could hardly speak. She and Fa are talking now, and it sounds as if she'll be coming as soon as she can."

"Oh, Sebastian ..." She stared at him with shining eyes. "I'm so glad you phoned her! That was so *brave* of you. That was as brave as Sir Lancelot!"

She shouldn't have said that!

But Sebastian smiled. "It *felt* as brave as Sir Lancelot, even though I'm not Sir Lancelot any more. Listen, Corrie, I want to apologize to you, too. I know I've been ignoring you. That's because you were my fellow knight and I was afraid to bring all that stuff up again."

"I'm not a knight any more," Corrie told him. "None of us are. The Round Table is over. I cleaned out Camelot and packed all the knight stuff into a box."

"That's just as well, although there's no reason the rest of you can't play the game. You're still young enough for it. Not like me."

"Did you really think you were the reincarnation of Sir Lancelot?" Corrie asked him.

"I really did for a while. Somehow I got off track. I just couldn't face Mum's death, and then losing Jennifer. It was all too painful." He swallowed hard. "Thanks, Corrie. If you and Fa hadn't rescued me I don't know what would have happened."

"You don't have to talk about it," said Corrie quickly.

"Well, I've certainly talked about it a lot with Dr. Samuel! I still do." Sebastian's eyes were clear and glowing. "I have so much to thank you for, Corrie. You've been so loyal all through this. And now look what you've done! You got me to apologize, which I just couldn't seem to do on my own. You're still my brave and loyal Gareth."

Corrie stood up and Sebastian engulfed her in a hug, pressing so hard that it hurt. She had never heard of knights hugging each other, but they were no longer knights of the Round Table. They were only a brother and sister who loved each other, and yet that was just as magic.

20

Molly

*I*n November, the show of Mum's paintings opened. It was called "Molly Bell: A Retrospective." Fa had let each of them choose one painting to keep. Corrie picked the one she used to call *Horses in the Rain*. Fa chose three. He had moved back into his and Mum's bedroom, and his paintings hung in there. The rest of them were scattered over the house, like jewels against the dark wood panelling.

Now Corrie stood proudly in the crowd at the opening night. The paintings were a rainbow of colours around the room. Each had a little tag below it with its title and cost. Some of the tags already had red dots on them, to show that those paintings had been sold.

Fa had let them choose the titles for the paintings that didn't have them. They had spent many evenings coming up with *Dancy Trees* (Juliet), *Happy* (Orly), *An Explosion of Fire* (Harry), and *In the Garden* (Aunt Madge). Roz had chosen *Let's Dance!* for one, and Sebastian had decided that a dark painting with bright swirly lines in one corner should be called *The Coming of Light*.

Many people were studying the paintings. Others were talking loudly and helping themselves to wine or cookies or pop.

Corrie tried not to rub her legs together. Tonight she was wearing nylons for the first time. Roz had helped her fasten each one to a garter belt. The clips on the belt dug uncomfortably into her thighs, and her legs felt trapped in the tight sheer fabric. But her black pumps looked elegant without socks.

Corrie's new blue twin-set matched her kilt, and her ponytail was tied with a matching blue ribbon. The rest of the family looked just as presentable. Fa was in the first new suit he had bought in six years, Sebastian was wearing a striped tie of Fa's, the twins and Harry were neat and clean, and Roz outshone them all in her pink chemise and fresh perm. Even Aunt Madge had a new dress instead of her usual stained one.

"*Corrie*, you're wearing *nylons*!" Meredith rushed up with her parents. "Mum, *please* can I get some?"

"Maybe for Christmas, darling," said Mrs. Cooper. "Corrie, your mother's paintings are amazing! We're going to buy one for our living room, the one called *Glow*."

"You are?" Then she could still see it! "I named that one," she said proudly.

Aunt Madge approached them, a twin dangling from each hand. "Now don't eat too much, Orly," she warned as he stuffed a cookie into his mouth with his free hand. "You've already had three. Isn't this delightful, Corrie? Dear Molly would be so pleased. Hello, Dot. How are you?"

She and Mrs. Cooper began to chat. Mr. Cooper took Meredith to meet someone, and Corrie went to get a drink. She sat on a chair and watched Fa across the room, surrounded by old friends of his and Mum's. Some of them hadn't seen him since she died, she heard them tell him. All around her people kept saying, "Molly would be so happy."

What if Mum could really be here? She would be thrilled and proud to see her paintings on display and to know how many were going to live in other people's homes, as if a bit of her were going there too. Most of all, she would ask how her family was.

We're all *fine*, Mum, thought Corrie. Aunt Madge had settled in so quickly, it was as if she'd never left. Fa had hired Mrs. Morrissey to clean the house, so Aunt Madge could concentrate on cooking and the twins. Corrie could go to her with her worries about how hard math was in junior high, or how she didn't want to go to the sock hops that happened every Friday. "It's all right, Corrie dear. You'll go when you're ready to. Don't you worry about what everyone else is doing," Aunt Madge had told her.

The twins treated Aunt Madge as if she were their real mother, going to her first with their needs instead of to the others. At first this bothered Corrie, but then she realized they had no memory of Mum. They were still "handfuls," as Aunt Madge called them, but with both Fa's and Aunt Madge's attention they were behaving much better at school.

Harry and his friend Peter had finished their rocket and were building a satellite in Peter's back yard. Harry smiled more now; he even let Aunt Madge tuck him into bed. That fall he'd asked Orly to help him take off the wheels from some old roller skates and screw them to a thick board. The two of them spent hours riding the board down the driveway, sparks flying beneath it. "My brother Harry and me have made a new invention!" Orly told everyone.

Roz was as busily involved with school as ever. She was the best baton thrower in grade nine. Corrie couldn't believe she was interested in something so silly. Being popular Roz's sister, however, gave her an edge at Laburnum. Older girls were kind to her and helped her find her way around.

Junior high was still scary, but it grew less so every week. At least Meredith was in her homeroom. Having different teachers for each subject was confusing, and Corrie had more homework than she'd ever had in her life. She missed Mr. Zelmach's easygoing teaching style; all her teachers at Laburnum were very strict, as if they were afraid that chaos would erupt if they weren't.

The best part of school so far had been a new fad. In October, the Hula-Hoop craze had hit Vancouver, and the schoolyard was a mass of whirling, coloured hoops. Corrie had asked Fa to buy her a yellow one. Meredith's was green. She could twirl more than a hundred times; Corrie had managed only forty-six so far. "That's because *I* have hips and you *don't*!" claimed Meredith.

Every hook in the cloakrooms was festooned with a colourful circle. Sometimes they fell down, and there were intense arguments about which was whose. Corrie and Meredith scratched their names in the plastic to make sure theirs weren't mixed up. Even the grade nines had them. Hula-Hoops made junior high more like elementary school, as if they could all be kids a little longer.

If Mum were here, she would be proudest of Sebastian. Corrie watched him listening intently to one of Mum's friends. They were probably talking about art. Sebastian was taking art at school and art lessons after school. Now he drew and painted outside his room, sketching trees and the house and even the family. No one could believe how good he was. "You've inherited Molly's talent, my boy," said Fa.

Sebastian still had to go to see Dr. Samuel, but now he went only once a month. He was attending the high school near the university instead of the one Jennifer and Terry went to. He took the bus every morning and came home with Fa in the late afternoons. He told Corrie that he liked his new school. He hadn't made any friends there yet, but at least it was a fresh start. No one knew him from before. No one knew that he used to have long hair or that he'd been bullied.

Occasionally Sebastian's eyes would go flat again and he'd drift away from the family. Most of the time, though, he was his old self, but a more relaxed version He seemed relieved to let Fa and Aunt Madge run the family. After a few awkward and silent days with Aunt Madge, he began cautiously talking to her again. Aunt Madge was careful not to intrude on his privacy, but he didn't seem to mind when she handed him his ironed shirts or reminded him to set the table.

"Are you having a good time, Corrie?" Sebastian slipped into the chair beside her. Her brother was so handsome in his grey suit, which matched his eyes. His hair was longer in front now, not as severely short as it had been in the summer. He looked so grown up.

"I'm having a *wonderful* time! Are you?"

He nodded. "I feel as if Mum is really here, don't you? She's here in her paintings, which means she'll never really die." He took her hand. "This is a very special night, Gareth."

Corrie was startled, but only for a second. Sebastian was just joking. The Round Table was over forever, but Corrie smiled at her perfect gentle knight.

ACKNOWLEDGEMENTS

For their good memories, advice, and encouragement, many thanks to Deirdre and Donna Baker, Chris Ellis, Sarah Ellis, Jamie Evrard, Ann Farris, Barbara Greeniaus, Ron Pearson, Bill Porteous, Judi Saltman, Ellen Visser, my editor David Kilgour, and especially Katherine Farris.